¡Arriba Baseball!

A Collection of Latino/a Baseball Fiction

edited by

Robert Paul Moreira

¡Arriba Baseball!

A Collection of Latino/a Baseball Fiction

edited by

Robert Paul Moreira

VAO publishing

DONNA, TX

Text copyright © 2013 VAO Publishing.
Cover image copyright © 2013 Jason Rey Pérez.

ISBN 10: 0615781837
ISBN 13: 978-0615781839

VAO Publishing
A division of Valley Artistic Outreach
4717 N FM 493
Donna, TX 78537
www.vaopublishing.com

First printed edition: May 2013

Contents

Contributor Biographies

Acknowledgements

"Uncle Rock" was first published in *The New Yorker* (2010) and is in *Before the End, after the Beginning* (Grove, 2011).

"Tomboy Forgiveness" first appeared in *Baseball Crazy: Ten Stories that Cover all the Bases,* edited by Nancy Mercado (Dial Books, 2008). It also appeared in *Heart Shaped Cookies and Other Stories* (Bilingual Press Review, 2011).

"Baseball over the Moon" originally appeared in a shorter version under the title "Growing up Tomboy" in *SWIRL: Literary Arts Journal* 12.1 (2010). Copyright © 2010 Kathryn Lane. Reprinted with permission of Kathryn Lane; the full-length story is included in *NewBorder: Contemporary Voices from the US/Mexico Border Anthology* (Texas A&M University Press, 2013).

"You'll Hit It over Anzaldúas Bridge" originally appeared in *SOL: English Writing in Mexico* (2011), and was subsequently reprinted in the print anthology *SOL: English Writing in Mexico*, Vol. I (2012).

"Good Father" received honorable mention in the 2011 *Texas Observer* Short Story Contest judged by Larry McMurtry.

Dedication

For Flores Moreira and Juan Cueto.

Foreword

In no field of American endeavor is invention more rampant than in baseball, whose whole history is a lie from beginning to end, from its creation myth to its rosy models of commerce, community and fair play. The game's epic feats and revered figures, its pieties about racial harmony and bleacher democracy, its artful blurring of sport and business—all of it is bunk, tossed up with a wink and a nudge.

—John Thorn, *Baseball in the Garden of Eden*

NOTHING AMONG BASEBALL'S CHERISHED SELF-PROMOTIONS has enjoyed more traction than the enticing dictum of French-born American historian Jacques Barzun. Barzun tells us (and hundreds who have quoted him remind us) that "whoever wants to know the heart and mind of America had better learn baseball." And yet just like the thinly-veiled lies about General Abner Doubleday and the game's Immaculate

Conception in the rural pastures Cooperstown, or all the pure hogwash about unique and native North American character traits imbedded in the sport of bats and balls, Barzun's seductive yet simplistic dictum is at best a distracting diversion and at worst an outright lie.

The truth of the matter is that it has always been precisely the other way around. One simply cannot fully grasp the rare spectacle of North American professional baseball without first owning a deep and studied appreciation for the American cultural milieu that nurtures, inspires and shapes the self-anointed "American national pastime." More simply put, baseball is not in any true sense a "transparent window" into either the American conscience or the dominant American culture. It is instead an "opaque mirror" that merely reflects the larger culture from which it emerges. Baseball (major league style) does not reveal America; it is rather the American psyche itself that explains the unique phenomenon of American baseball.

There is perhaps no more lucid illustration of baseball as cultural mirror and societal reflection than that provided by the leading alternative universe of professional baseball—the one found in Japan. Robert Whiting has devoted several volumes to exploring and explaining precisely how the diamond sport as it is played in the Land of the Rising Sun has been radically modified from its original American model across eight decades to accommodate and replicate Japanese social values. Watching a Japanese professional game in Tokyo or Kobe or Fukuoka will provide the Western mind with preciously little insight into the subtleties of a highly complex and ritualized Japanese culture. But a deeper familiarity with the Japanese people and their tradition-wrapped nation will surely explain much about baseball as it is played Samurai Style. The ingrained Japanese emphasis upon group identity, public cooperation, relentless hard work, unwavering respect for age and seniority, the importance of saving face in all situations, and above all xenophobic nationalism—these are the elements crucial to appreciating and even comprehending the way the Japanese people approaching their own adopted "national pastime." Baseball hardly explains Japan, but Japanese history and Japanese cultural identity go far toward explaining Japanese baseball.

The same is true in that other baseball epicenter found in the island nations of the Caribbean. Contrary to what many careless historians have suggested, baseball was not brought to its Caribbean cradle in Cuba by American marines in 1866; it had already been transported to Havana several years earlier by a pair of teenage native sons. It was the Guilló brothers (Nemesio and Ernesto) who carried the equipment and rules of the game back to their homeland from Alabama, where they had become enchanted with the novel sport as visiting prep school students. It is true enough that Cubans—embroiled in a lengthy battle for independence from Spain—admired all things North American and saw baseball play as a comfortable alternative to bullfighting and other social institutions so strongly identified with the burdensome traditions of their cultural and political Spanish oppressors. But the Cubans also quickly imposed upon the game their own native flavor and flamboyant style and then transported it to numerous early twentieth-century sugar plantation outposts in Venezuela, Puerto Rico, the Dominican Republic, and even eastern Mexico. It was the Cubans and not the Americans who were the late-nineteenth and early-twentieth century apostles of baseball in other Latin American nations.

It is in the very ethnic foundations of North America's professional game that we see the starkest examples of baseball as cultural mirror rather than cultural definer. The early half of the twentieth century was an era of massive immigration into the United States and most of that immigration came in successive waves from first Western Europe (the Irish and Germans), and later more Southern (the Italians) and Eastern (the Slavs and Greeks) outposts. Those hordes of immigrants found the wildly popular national game of baseball to be a key to their American assimilation—both as ballplayers and fans. But successive waves of immigrant ballplayers transformed and altered the American game every bit as much or even more than they ever adapted to it.

Names like McGraw, Keeler, Kelley, Ewing, Schaefer and Donovan constitute the bulk of entries in the baseball encyclopedias recording the history of the game from the decades before the first great world war. Irishmen (Connie Mack, Pat Moran, Joe McGinnity, Dan Brouthers) were the backbone of big league rosters in the 1890s, followed closely by swingers and chuckers of Anglo-Saxon and Germanic stock. The famed Baltimore Orioles of the 1890s, for example, posted a lineup that looked like the Irish national all-stars: Ned Hanlon, John McGraw, Willie Keeler, Hugh Jennings, Joe Kelley, and Kid Gleason among others. Germans of the era were represented by such prominent figures as Honus Wagner and Dutch (later called Casey) Stengel. The great Babe Ruth and slugging Lou Gehrig were also cut from stoutly German immigrant stock. Finally there were broad nosed Italians in the 1930s and 1940s—the DiMaggios, Lazzari, Crosetti, Rizzuto, Garagiola, and Berra—and the Poles and other Slavs—the pitching Coveleski brothers, Al Simmons (born Aloysius Szymanski), Musial, Sauer, Zernial and so many muscle-bound sluggers from the coalfields of West Virginia and Pennsylvania.

But despite all this ethnic influx, the professional baseball known to the bulk of the nation and its sporting press remained a purely white and ruthlessly segregated affair; men of color and those with African roots were forced to play in their own banished leagues hidden from the mainstream culture. The American baseball of the first half of the recent century was as racially divided, and thus as painfully undemocratic and driven by social injustice, as the larger American culture that housed it. The America of our post-modern era has morphed into a very different land—a multicultural and multiethnic haven with deep-seated divisions and stark religious, racial, ethnic and political divides that have not only polarized but in large part paralyzed the nation's current political and social scene.

And once more there is no better reflection of the new American scene than the world of major league baseball, where today nearly 30% of all big league roster slots are manned not by naturalized immigrants (as in the past) but rather by mercenary athletes from Latin America and Asia. (The specific numbers for the recent 2012 season are 26.9% Latinos, 1.9% Asians, 7.2% Afro-Americans, and 63.9% White Americans; this contrasts with 90.7% White American big leaguers and only 3.7% Latino imports in 1954.) Baseball today has become every bit as ethnically diverse as the American nation that houses it. And some might argue that to some extent this explains the sport's recent slide behind NFL football and NBA basketball (both more "American" in their ballplayer populations) as the spectacle of choice for a mainstream majority-class television viewing public.

The fifteen stories presented in this anthology—penned largely but not exclusively by Latino and Latina authors—reflect a contemporary American baseball reality in which droves of Hispanic and Asian immigrant families now cheer lustily for their own ethnic heroes from the original homeland and in which for more than a quarter-century Latino stars (and to a lesser extent a handful of Asian imports) have stood among the game's biggest heroes—slugger Albert Pujols from the Dominican Republic, triple crown winner Miguel Cabrera from Venezuela, Cuba's Orlando "El Duque" Hernández, Puerto Rico's Ivan Rodríguez, and so many more. These are thus not at all the typical baseball stories of a past century, celebrating the sandlot game of a Southern rural white America. And the fact that this is in part a bilingual anthology reflects a world in which baseball with its new international trappings has largely become a truly multi-lingual game.

Pitcher-turned-author Jim Bouton provided us with one of the most lucid if paradoxical facets of a sport that has long maintained so firm a hold on the American (and Latin American and Asian) psyche. In his classic autobiographical volume *Ball Four* Bouton mused that "you spend a good piece of your life gripping a baseball and in the end it turns out that it was the other way around all the time." We might well pause here to reflect that in the case of Jacques Barzun's so-often misapplied lines baseball has simply thrown us yet another deceptive curve ball. We have too long accepted Barzun's notion that one needs to learn about baseball in order to appreciate the cultural and historic definitions of America and of Americans, when in truth it turns out that it was the other way around all the time.

— Peter C. Bjarkman

Introduction

A COLLEAGUE OF MINE RECENTLY WENT TO SEE BRIAN Hegeland's film *42*, which recounts Jackie Robinson's historic entry into Major League Baseball. The scenes that illustrated the blatant racism and segregation of the epoch "made me wanna cry," she detailed in her mid-afternoon text message, and I pictured her sitting comfortably in one of the local Carmike or Tinseltown theaters, a tub of well-buttered popcorn on her lap, silently wiping her tears away among the rest of the spectators. Already dreaming of my own tub of cooked kernels, I decided that tomorrow I would take a well-deserved day off from my doctoral rationales to go and see the latest sports movie that was making such a buzz.

Without giving too much away for those who have not yet seen the film, *42* does an exceptional job of detailing Robinson's frustrations as he, under the tutelage of Brooklyn Dodgers's owner Branch Rickey (played masterfully by Harrison Ford), seeks to upend organized baseball's established color line. The movie is without a doubt a testament to the determination of two men willing to risk their reputations and lives for change. In *42*, Robinson (played by Chadwick Boseman) performs as the ultimate Hollywood hero, a permutation of the cinematic version of *The Natural's* beleaguered yet heroic Roy Hobbs, rounding the bases with much more than personal statistics on the line. In true Hollywood glitz and glare, Hegeland's biopic offers up exactly what audiences have always paid money to see: one man fighting against, and ultimately overcoming, an unjust system.

And yet Robinson was never alone in this struggle, nor was he the first choice to integrate organized baseball in the United States. Native American ballplayers such as Louis Sockalexis and Charles "Chief" Bender had been scrambling across infields and straddling pitching mounds as early as 1897 in Cleveland and Philadelphia, respectively. Moreover, historians Samuel Regalado, Rob Ruck, Peter Bjarkman, Adrian Burgos, and others have detailed how both dark and light-skinned Latinos also populated baseball diamonds during these racially-fueled times in the U.S. Along with Native Americans, Latino ballplayers including Esteban Bellán, Armando Marsans, and Adolfo Luque performed successfully for their respective clubs (Luque pitched for the Cincinnati Reds during the 1919 World Series, for instance), forcing baseball owners to justify their existences within this exclusively Anglo space, and ultimately complicating the racial perceptions and policies of the era. While Jackie Robinson's entry into organized baseball was without a doubt fraught with its prejudices, physical altercations, and even death threats, there is no doubt that his ingress into the 1947 Brooklyn Dodgers's lineup would not have been possible had it not been for those who tested the Jim Crow policies before him. Scholars have also indicated that Branch Rickey had contemplated a dark-skinned, Cuban ballplayer by the name of Silverio García well before the name of Jackie Robinson ever surfaced, but eventually abandoned the idea due to García's intolerance for racial insults. None of these facts are mentioned in the film *42*, nor is the significance of the All'American Girls Professional Baseball League (founded in 1943), in which Latinas such as Isabel "Lefty" Álvarez, Eulalia Gonzáles, and Margaret "Poncho" Villa performed admirably and complicated their own distinct set of unjust perceptions[1]. In true Hollywood expediency, Hegeland's film portrays Branch Rickey as the quintessential American luminary seeking to integrate baseball within a nation populated by two groups only: Anglos and African Americans. In its own way, this collection pays homage to all those who suffered beneath the racial vitriol prior to Jackie Robinson.

My idea for *¡Arriba Baseball!* surfaced well before Hegeland's film, of course. But *42* is just one more example

---

[1] The All-American Girls Professional Baseball League (AAGPBL) existed from 1943 to 1954. In 1992, Penny Marshall's film *A League of Their Own* re-introduced American audiences to the women of the AAGPBL and to their significant contributions to the survival of organized baseball in the United States in the wake of WWII. Gai Berlage's *Women in Baseball: The Forgotten History* (1994) provides a thorough analysis of the role of women involved in the sport. Thanks also go to Mario Longoria for his research and for providing the names of the AAGPBL Latina ballplayers mentioned above.

of the Latino erasure that seems to permeate American history and popular culture. I began with a simple question, actually: *Does Latino/a-authored baseball fiction even exist?* I posed this question to myself as my doctoral studies dealing with constructions of difference in sports developed and I began to read countless short fiction and novels by the likes of Ring Lardner, Stuart Dybek, Lamar Herrin, T.C. Boyle, W.P. Kinsella, Eric Rolfe Greenberg, Bernard Malamud and so many others. While some of the fiction did include Latino characters (Malamud's *The Natural*, for instance, includes a Mexican center fielder named Juan Flores), only a handful had been penned by Latino authors. The lack of female authorship in the genre was even more staggering, with Latina writers nearly nonexistent. Given the popularity of baseball throughout Mexico and Latin America, the last three World Baseball Classic tournaments, as well as with the success of so many Latinos in Major League Baseball, it seemed odd to me that so few Latino/a authors were contemplating the game creatively, or at the very least that I was having such a difficult time locating these types of texts. The stage was thus set for this collection, and I became determined to do all I could to find these stories and share them with others.

My goal with *¡Arriba Baseball!* was to do away with any and all notions of gendered and white privilege in baseball literature, as well as to counter the idea that Latino/a authors have little or nothing to contribute to the genre. I believe this collection has accomplished that and so much more. The fifteen stories in this anthology are not the products of the traditional pastoral nostalgia for the game that helped conjure Lardner's "Alibi Ike," for instance, or Malamud's Roy Hobbs, Herrin's Dick Dixon, or Kinsella's enchanted cornfield in Iowa. Instead, all of the stories in this collection succeed in (re)defining the game of baseball and all its nuances through the prisms of Latino/a experience, craft, and imagination. Just like the Native American and Latino ballplayers that disrupted the virulent lines of apartheid and segregation in organized baseball before them, the authors of *¡Arriba Baseball!* are also transgressing, but into a literary permutation of that once-restricted historical space, swinging for the fences with language, imagery, memories, and dreams. After all, to throw his infamous screwball, Fernando "El Toro" Valenzuela needed to learn to grip the baseball first in his village in Navajoa, Sonora, Mexico; and it is only in movements and crossings such as these that erasures and unfair perceptions will ever be contested. *Arriba Baseball!* is by no means the start of this synergy of historiography, experience, and creativity, and I pray it is not the end either. I offer it up to everyone as that perpetual moment at the apex of any and all well-hit home runs, stuck in endless blue skies, beneath which the games are for all and last forever.

Meanwhile, as this anthology seeks to overcome textual boundaries through its literary creations, Latino ballplayers continue to emphasize their indelible marks on and off the field of play. In March of this year, the team representing the Dominican Republic won the third installment of the World Baseball Classic tournament for the first time. This powerhouse team included ballplayers such as New York

Yankees' second baseman Robinson Canó, Blue Jays' shortstop José Reyes, and Cleveland Indians' catcher Carlos Santana. Fans of the game will also remember closer Fernando Rodney's ninth-inning dominance and, of course, his "rally plantain" that became his signature prop during the entire tournament.

And now the 2013 Major League Baseball season is well underway, and no one is performing more admirably than Venezuelan Miguel Cabrera. The Detroit Tigers' first baseman is on a torrid pace to outperform his offensive statistics from the 2012 season where he compiled a .330 batting average, hit 44 home runs, and drove in 139 runs. The first Latino to win MLB's prestigious Triple Crown Award (best batting average, most home runs, most runs-batted-in), Cabrera is also the first player to receive that distinction since Carl Yastrzemski of the Boston Red Sox in 1967. As of last night, Cabrera has 12 home runs; he will no doubt hit many more. Cap on, waving my own plantain, I present you with the fifteen long-balls in this collection. May they take you up, up, over every fence...and beyond.

¡Arriba!
Robert Paul Moreira, Editor

Uncle Rock

by Dagoberto Gilb

I N THE MORNING, AT HIS FAVORITE RESTAURANT, ERICK got to order his favorite American food, sausage and eggs and hash-brown *papitas* fried crunchy on top. He'd be sitting there, eating with his mother, not bothering anybody, and life was good, when a man started changing it all. Lots of times it was just a man staring too much—but then one would come over. Friendly, he'd put his thick hands on the table as if he were touching water, and squat low, so that he was at sitting level, as though he were so polite, and he'd smile, with coffee-and-tobacco-stained teeth. He might wear a bolo tie and speak in a drawl. Or he might have on a tan uniform, a company logo on the back, an oval name patch on the front. Or he'd be in a nothing-special work shirt, white or striped, with a couple of pens clipped onto the left side pocket, tucked into a pair of jeans or chinos that were morning-clean still, with a pair of scuffed work boots that laced up higher than regular shoes. He'd say something about her earrings, or her bracelet, or her hair, or her eyes, and if she had on her white uniform how nice it looked on her. Or he'd come right out with it and tell her how pretty she was, how he couldn't keep himself from walking up, speaking to her directly, and could they talk again? Then he'd wink at Erick. Such a fine-looking boy! How old is he, eight or nine? Erick wasn't even small for an eleven-year-old. He tightened his jaw then, slanted his eyes up from his plate at his mom and not the man, definitely not this man he did not care for. Erick drove a fork into a goopy American egg yolk and bled it into his American potatoes. She wouldn't offer the man Erick's correct age either, saying only that he was growing too fast.

She almost always gave the man her number if he was wearing a suit. Not a sports coat but a buttoned suit with a starched white shirt and a pinned tie meant something to her. Once in a while, Erick saw one of these men again at the front door of the apartment in Silverlake. The man winked at Erick as if they were buddies. Grabbed his shoulder or arm, squeezed the muscle against the bone. What did Erick want to be when he grew up? A cop, a jet-airplane mechanic, a travel agent, a court reporter? A dog groomer? Erick stood there, because his mom said that he shouldn't be impolite. His mom's date said he wanted to take Erick along with them sometime. The three of them. What kind of places did Erick think were fun? Erick said nothing. He never said anything when the men were around, and not because of his English, even if that was what his mother implied to explain his silence. He didn't talk to any of the men and he didn't talk much to his mom either. Finally they took off, and Erick's night was his alone. He raced to the grocery store and bought half a gallon of chocolate ice cream. When he got back, he turned on the TV, scooted up real close, as close as he could, and ate his dinner with a soup spoon. He was away from all the men. Even though a man had given the TV to them. He was a salesman in an appliance store who'd bragged that a rich customer had given it to him and so why shouldn't he give it to Erick's mom, who couldn't afford such a good TV otherwise?

When his mom was working as a restaurant hostess, and was going to marry the owner, Erick ate hot-fudge sundaes and drank chocolate shakes. When she worked at a trucking company, the owner of all the trucks told her he was getting a divorce. Erick climbed into the rigs, with their rooms full of dials and levers in the sky. Then she started working in an engineer's office. There was no food or fun there, but even he could see the money. He was not supposed to touch anything, but what was there to touch—the tubes full of paper? He and his mom were invited to the engineer's house, where he had two horses and a stable, a swimming pool, and two convertible sports cars. The engineer's family was there: his grown children, his gray-haired parents. They all sat down for dinner in a dining room that seemed bigger than Erick's apartment, with three candelabras on the table, and a tablecloth and cloth napkins. Erick's mom took him aside to tell him to be well mannered at the table and polite to everyone. Erick hadn't said anything. He never spoke anyway, so how could he have said anything wrong? She leaned into his ear and said that she wanted them to know that he spoke English. That whole dinner he was silent, chewing quietly, taking the smallest bites, because he didn't want them to think he liked their food.

When she got upset about days like that, she told Erick that she wished they could just go back home. She was tired of worrying. "Back," for Erick, meant mostly the stories he'd heard from her, which never sounded so good to him: She'd had to share a room with her brothers and sisters. They didn't have toilets. They didn't have electricity. Sometimes they didn't have enough food. He saw this Mexico as if it were the backdrop of a movie on afternoon TV, where children walked around barefoot in the dirt or on broken sidewalks and small men wore wide-brimmed straw hats and baggy white shirts and pants. The women went to church all the time and prayed to alcoved saints and, heads down, fearful, counted rosary beads. There were rocks everywhere, and scorpions and tarantulas and rattlesnakes, and vultures and no trees and not much water, and skinny dogs and donkeys, and ugly bad guys with guns and bullet vests who rode laughing into town to drink and shoot off their pistols and rifles, driving their horses all over like dirt bikes on desert dunes. When they spoke English, they had stupid accents— his mom didn't have an accent like theirs. It didn't make sense to him that Mexico would only be like that, but what if it was close? He lived on paved, lighted city streets, and a bicycle ride away were the Asian drugstore and the Armenian grocery store and the corner where black Cubans drank coffee and talked Dodgers baseball.

When he was in bed, where he sometimes prayed, he thanked God for his mom, who he loved, and he apologized for not talking to her, or to anyone, really, except his friend Albert, and he apologized for her never going to church and for his never taking Holy Communion, as Albert did—though only to God would he admit that he wanted to only because Albert did. He prayed for good to come, for his mom and for him, since God was like magic, and happiness might come the way of early morning, in the trees and bushes full of sparrows next to his open window, louder and louder when he listened hard, eyes closed.

THE ENGINEER WOULDN'T HAVE MATTERED IF ERICK HADN'T told Albert that he was his dad. Albert had just moved into the apartment next door and lived with both his mother and his father, and since Albert's mother already didn't like Erick's mom, Erick told him that his new dad was an engineer. Erick actually believed it, too, and thought that he might even get his own horse. When that didn't happen, and his mom was lying on her bed in the middle of the day, blowing her nose, because she didn't have the job anymore, that was when Roque came around again. Roque was nobody—or he was anybody. He wasn't special, he wasn't not. He tried to speak English to Erick, thinking that was the reason Erick didn't say anything when he was there. And Erick had to tell Albert that Roque was his uncle, because the engineer was supposed to be his new dad any minute. Uncle Rock, Erick said. His mom's brother, he told Albert. Roque worked at night and was around during the day, and one day he offered Erick and Albert a ride. When his mom got in the car, she scooted all the way over to Roque on the bench seat. Who was supposed to be her brother, Erick's Uncle Rock. Albert didn't say anything, but he saw what had happened, and that was it for Erick. Albert had parents, grandparents, and a brother and a sister, and he'd hang out only when one of his cousins wasn't coming by. Erick didn't need a friend like him.

What if she married Roque, his mom asked him one day soon afterward. She told Erick that they would move away from the apartment in Silverlake to a better neighborhood. He did want to move, but he wished that it weren't because of Uncle Rock. It wasn't just because Roque didn't have a swimming pool or horses or a big ranch house. There wasn't much to criticize except that he was always too willing and nice, too considerate, too generous. He wore nothing flashy or expensive, just ordinary clothes that were clean and ironed, and shoes he kept shined. He combed and parted his hair neatly. He didn't have a buzzcut like the men who didn't like kids. He moved slow, he talked slow, as quiet as night. He only ever said yes to Erick's mom. How could she not like him for that? He loved her so much—anybody could see his pride when he was with her. He signed checks and gave her cash. He knocked on their door carrying cans and fruit and meat. He was there when she asked, gone when she asked, back whenever, grateful. He took her out to restaurants on Sunset, to the movies in Hollywood, or on drives to the beach in rich Santa Monica.

ROQUE KNEW THAT ERICK LOVED BASEBALL. DID ROQUE LIKE baseball? It was doubtful that he cared even a little bit—he didn't listen to games on the radio or TV, and he never looked at a newspaper. He loved boxing though. He knew the names of all the Mexican fighters as if they lived here, as if they were Dodgers players like Steve Yeager, Dusty Baker, Kenny Landreaux or Mike Marshall, Pedro Guerrero. Roque did know about Fernando Valenzuela, everyone did, even his mom, which is why she agreed to let Roque take them to a game. What Mexican didn't love Fernando? Dodger Stadium was close to their apartment. He'd been there once with Albert and his family—well, outside it, on a nearby hill, to see the fireworks for Fourth of July. His mom decided that all three of them would go on a Saturday afternoon, since Saturday night, Erick thought, she might want to go somewhere else, even with somebody else.

Roque, of course, didn't know who the Phillies were. He knew nothing about the strikeouts by Steve Carlton or the home runs by Mike Schmidt. He'd never heard of Pete Rose. It wasn't that Erick knew very much either, but there was nothing that Roque could talk to him about, if they were to talk.

If Erick showed his excitement when they drove up to Dodger Stadium and parked, his mom and Roque didn't really notice it. They sat in the bleachers, and for him the green of the field was a magic light; the stadium decks surrounding them seemed as far away as Rome. His body was somewhere it had never been before. The fifth inning? That's how late they were. Or were they right on time, because they weren't even sure they were sitting in the right seats yet when he heard the crack of the bat , saw the crowd around them rising as it came at them. Erick saw the ball. He had to stand and move and stretch his arms and want that ball until it hit his bare hands and stayed there. Everybody saw him catch it with no bobble. He felt all the eyes and voices around him as if they were every set of eyes and every voice in the stadium. His mom was saying something, and Roque, too, and then, finally, it was just him and that ball and his stinging hands. He wasn't even sure if it had been hit by Pete Guerrero. He thought for sure it had been, but he didn't ask. He didn't watch the game then—he couldn't. He didn't care who won. He stared at his official National League ball, reimagining what had happened. He ate a hot dog and drank a soda and he sucked the salted peanuts and the wooden spoon from his chocolate-malt ice cream. He rubbed the bumpy seams of his home run ball.

Game over, they were the last to leave. People were hanging around, not going straight to their cars. Roque didn't want to leave. He didn't want to end it so quickly, Erick thought, while he still had her with him. Then one of the Phillies came out of the stadium door and people swarmed— boys mostly, but also men and some women and girls—and they got autographs before the player climbed onto the team's bus. Joe Morgan, they said. Then Garry Maddox appeared. Erick clutched the ball but he didn't have a pen. He just watched, his back to the gray bus the Phillies were getting into.

Then a window slid open. *Hey, big man*, a voice said. Erick really wasn't sure. *Gimme the ball, la pelota*, the face in the bus said. *I'll have it signed, comprendes? Échalo, just toss it to me.* Erick obeyed. He tossed it up to the hand that was reaching out. The window closed. The ball was gone a while, so long that his mom came up to him, worried that he'd lost it. The window slid open again and the voice spoke to her. *We got the ball, Mom. It's not lost, just a few more.* When the window opened once more, this time the ball was there. *Catch.* There were all kinds of signatures on it, though none that he could really recognize except for Joe Morgan and Pete Rose.

Then the voice offered more, and the hand threw something at him. *For your mom, okay? Comprendes?* Erick stared at the asphalt lot where the object lay, as if he'd never seen a folded-up piece of paper before. *Para tu mamá, bueno?* He picked it up, and he started to walk over to his mom and Roque, who were so busy talking they hadn't noticed anything. Then he stopped. He opened the note himself. No one had said he couldn't read it. It said, *I'd like to get to know you. You are muy linda. Very beautiful and sexy. I don't speak Spanish very good, may be you speak better English, pero No Importa. Would you come by tonite and let me buy you a drink?* There was a phone number and a hotel room number. A name, too. A name that came at him the way that the home run had.

Erick couldn't hear. He could see only his mom ahead of him. She was talking to Roque, Roque was talking to her. Roque was the proudest man, full of joy because he was with her. It wasn't his fault he wasn't an engineer. Now Erick could hear again. Like sparrows hunting seed, boys gathered round the bus, calling out, while the voice in the bus was yelling at him, *Hey, big guy! Give it to her!* Erick had the ball in one hand and the note in the other. By the time he reached his mom and Roque, the note was already somewhere on the asphalt parking lot. *Look,* he said in a full voice. *They all signed my ball.*

Los Tecolotes

by Norma Elia Cantú

IT WAS ONE OF THOSE THINGS *DEL DESTINO*. **MEANT TO** be. In the stars. *La mano poderosa. Los dioses y las diosas.* The fates. Whatever it was, it was as it should have been, and it was. Or so Elizabeth, La Betty claimed. She was my mom's best friend so I heard the story often. Always with a morale attached to it. But did I listen? Of course not! *Así es la vida.* We are supposed to learn from our elders. Supposed to benefit from their mistakes. Or at least Betty always said it was a mistake, but I don't think so. How can a love story be a mistake?

It happened one warm spring evening during spring break, in fact. Elizabeth, or Betty as she was known, was a junior at a university up north; she chose it because it was far away as she could get from her South Texas home. Let's say that it was a private Catholic university in New Jersey, Anne Seton Hall University or some such. Well, anyway, she was up there away from family and friends *de una terquedad*, because when she was a senior in high school her best friend got engaged. Yes, at 16! And had a party and all, right after the George Washington's Birthday celebration and before her high school graduation *de las Ursulinas*, the Catholic girls school all the daughters of the *gente decente* attended in that small border town where only those who could afford going out of town went to college. We didn't get a university until decades later. In time for Betty's' daughters to attend.

She always remembered that warm spring day, when home for Spring Break, she went with her mother and father to the Tecolotes game as they often did during the season to the Parque La Junta in Nuevo Laredo. Los Tecolotes was their team, although they lived in Laredo, Texas. Her father was a fan from childhood. He remembered when the team was called La Junta and how it became *los Tecolotes*. It was a fitting name, the Owls, because they always played at night. Later in the 1980s the team would belong to both Laredo AND Nuevo Laredo and play in Mexico and in the US, too.

That afternoon they were playing a team from Veracruz, *los Águilas*, the Eagles. She found it interesting that the teams were named after birds and she mused about this and other things as she sat in the warm evening breeze under the bright lights. She was wearing a cool cotton dress, blue gingham edged with white rick rack along the neckline and the hemline. The crinoline in the style of the times made her small waist seem even tinier. She felt beautiful with her long shoulder long wavy auburn brown hair. Her green eyes sparkled and her red, red lipstick gave her the movie star glamour she hoped for.

IN THE DUSTY BASEBALL FIELD WHERE THEY WERE, WITH THE bright lights as the afternoon turned to evening, her destiny was changed forever. Just like in a movie. He was an outfielder, and a pretty good batter, too. When she first saw him way out there in left field, she just knew that he was the one. She whispered to Teresa, her sister, Who's the guy in left field? I don't know, Teresa answered, he must be new because I have never seen him before, wonder if he's any good. Just then as if to answer their questions he caught a high ball to left field easily and smoothly as when Betty played catch with her younger brother. She leaned in and whispered in Teresa's ear, I'm going to marry him. The announcer gave her the name of her future husband, father of her children. Pablo Soler caught that fly for a third out. The game was over and she craned her neck to see him loping to the dugout with his team, victorious and happy. Her heart skipped a beat when she thought he had caught her eye. But it can't be, she told herself. He's too far away to notice me.

THE NEXT NIGHT, ON SATURDAY, BETTY WENT TO THE MOVIES, *al* Rialto, with her sister and her boyfriend and some other friends. And who should appear but Pablo Soler, the baseball player from Veracruz who was with a few of his buddies.

Betty never gave us a year, but it must've been the mid or late 50s. I did the math. Yes, she was 21 when she married and that would make it 1957. Not many Chicanas were in college then. Fewer still were at private Catholic universities unless they were Latin Americans with a lot of money.

On Sunday she went back up north to her school routine and thought the budding romance would soon be over. He was so much older, she thought he would soon tire of the *pocha* everyone called *Güera*. A whole 5 years older! She was barely 20 and he was already 25. But he was so dreamy! *Un mango de manila*, as they would say back then for a very handsome man. And he spoke a dreamy Spanish with a slight lilt as they do in Veracruz. She wrote letters almost every night, hardly concentrated on her school work. She was a junior and would graduate in a year. He was traveling all over; when they met the season was just starting and it would not end until the playoffs in August. She hoped they would make it till then. But his team didn't make it to the playoffs. Everyone was captivated by the Little League team that year, *Los Industriales* from Monterrey who came to be known as the Little Giants, *los grandes gigantes*; they won the championship led by a tiny kid who chewed gum incessantly and was ambidextrous pitching and hitting equally well both ways. Ángel Macías pitched a *perfect game* for Monterrey and won the day. Mexico was jubilant.

Betty always mentions this fact when she tells the story of her romance with Pablo Soler who became the father of her children, indeed. She had eight children. She didn't finish college because when she came home that year, he came and asked for her hand in marriage. Are you sure, her father asked. *Sí, Papi*, he's the one, she answered.

They were married in November. He was already in training and she hardly saw him. They lived near his parents' house in Veracruz, near a church whose bells tolled every hour on the hour and nearly drove Betty crazy. *Me volvía loca*, she explains when she tells the story, to hear those bells!

But Pablo was not just gone for long periods during the season, he also began to drink. Then one season in the 60s, he came back to Veracruz when he finally recognized he could no longer play ball or dream of going to the big leagues in the US. His baseball days were over.

He opened a business with his father's help and did alright. The petroleum industry was nationalized and he became wealthy selling industrial equipment for a US firm. Betty helped with translating and with keeping the books. She had not majored in business in college but had taken a couple of accounting classes, plus she was pretty good with numbers. With the children, the business and all the social commitments she had in that town where it seemed everyone knows everyone and she was always the outsider, she never felt at home. But she learned to cook using *hoja santa* and other regional herbs not common in south Texas cooking. But overcome with homesickness and loneliness, one day she realized that she didn't love Pablo. She had loved the baseball player, but he was no longer there. Instead it was a stranger who came to her bed almost every night. She knew he had a lover and tolerated the lies until she could do so no more. The big fight was over the *Águilas*, in fact. They were playing the *Tecos* in Veracruz and she wanted to go see the game, but he wouldn't allow it. She was pregnant and she should stay home. But she defied him and showed up at the game with her young son and daughter. But as soon as they paid their tickets and entered the baseball park, she saw him. He casually had his arm on a woman's shoulder. His friends all around. The woman, a red head, Betty readily assumed was his lover. What humiliation! She turned around and to the dismay of her kids went right back home and began packing. She went to her in-laws' house to phone her father and ask that he send her money so she could go home with the kids. He did and she did. At this point, Betty usually sheds a tear or two and suddenly becomes that young 21-year old who looked out into the baseball field and saw her *destino*, her destiny, a tall handsome ball player who ran and expertly caught the ball as if plucking the moon from the sky.

Chasing Chato

by Wayne Rapp

HAVE YOU EVER HEARD OF **CHATO BELLO**? **IF YOU** are a Mexican baseball fan, you should know about this guy. Gustavo "Chato" Bello pitched the first perfect game in the history of Mexican professional baseball. That was in 1946. I didn't get to see him pitch until 1948 when he was with the Tampico *Alijadores*, and they were playing the San Luis Potosí *Tuneros*.

It was my fifteenth birthday, and I had talked my father into making the trip to see the game. The problem was that he also took my uncle Pelón, and the two of them got very drunk. I had wanted to stay after the game to see if I could get Chato's autograph, but the *borrachos* insisted on leaving early to see a bullfight. I had no choice but to go too, because I had to drive.

"Chato, Chato, Chato. That's all I hear out of you. He's not the only guy who plays baseball, you know," my father said in the car.

"He's the only one who ever pitched a perfect game in Mexico."

"You believe that shit? It's just like the fights. It was his turn. They let him do it. Tell him, Pelón."

Uncle Pelón was in the back seat, the sound of snoring and of his head bouncing off the window with every bump I hit the only noise coming from his direction.

"You never want to bet on those baseball games. They got 'em all fixed any time they want to. That's why I go to the bullfights. No way to get the bull to take a dive."

"If it was just Chato's turn, how come nobody ever had a turn before him or after him?"

"When the money's right, they will," he said, and that was the end of that.

In the years that closely followed, it became harder to become a professional baseball player in Mexico. Players from the Negro League in *los Estados Unidos* and also players from Cuba were coming into *la Liga Mexicana de Beisbol* in great numbers. Some of the Mexican players were leaving and going north to *los Estados Unidos* for more opportunity to make a team. I heard that Chato was one of those playing on the other side of the border.

I was becoming a pretty good baseball player myself—an infielder—but Chato Bello was still my hero. You had to be a very good player to even get a tryout, but by the time I was nineteen, I had a few teams that took a look at me. I even had a tryout with Tampico, Chato's old team, but they were looking for a power-hitting outfielder, not a slick-fielding infielder.

In 1951, I hooked up finally with a team that was barnstorming through northern Mexico. We would play a game or two in a town and then move on. At the end of the season, I was in Cananea, Sonora, when the team broke up. We didn't even get a bus ticket home. Just got dumped. Someone told me that Cananea was an Apache word that meant *horse meat*. I thought that was what I would be pretty quick if I didn't get a job. One of the guys said he heard the mines were hiring. He was right, and a few of us stayed on in Cananea to be copper miners. The work was hard and dirty, but it was nice to get a regular paycheck.

When that first winter passed, and spring came, I heard that Cananea was going to have a town baseball team. I wanted to get out in the field again and throw a baseball around, catch some ground balls, and get in the batter's box to hit a few. They had a couple of tryouts after work during the week then asked a group of us to come back on Sunday before they made the final cuts.

I was feeling pretty good about my chances of playing baseball for the Cananea team that summer. I wasn't one to brag, but I had been playing long enough to know that I was one of the best players on the field.

All the while we were working out I noticed an older guy hanging around watching. He was dark but didn't really look Mexican. I was pretty sure he was a *gringo*. He had been standing and talking to our manager while I was in the batting cage. I stung a couple pretty good ones right on a line into left field.

The *gringo* walked up to the cage while I was batting. "Hey, *chamaco*," he said. "Let me see you hit one to the opposite field." I hit the next one into the right field gap. And the one after that just to show him I could do it when I wanted to.

"You should be hitting there more. You're pulling too many pitches to left field. Pretty soon that's where they play you." He was definitely *gringo*, but there was nothing wrong with his Spanish.

"When you finish, come talk to me," he said and walked back to my manager.

I took a couple more cuts—hit them both to right field—and got out of the cage. As soon as I did, my buddy, Ishmael Marioqui, one of the guys I barnstormed with, was right in front of me. "What did he say?"

"Just wants to talk."

"Didn't you hear who he was?"

"No. Who is he?"

"He's a manager from *los Estados Unidos* looking for ballplayers. He's a famous guy up there. He was a pitcher in the Big Leagues, and he struck out Babe Ruth."

"Big joke," I said.

"No joke, man. If he takes you, see if he'll take me, too."

I looked away from Ishmael to see the *gringo* waving at me.

"Hey, *chamaco*, I don't have all day. Come over here."

I trotted over to him, more out of respect for his age than anything.

My manager said, "Beto, this is Mr. Syd Cohen. He has a ball team in Arizona, and he wants to talk to you about playing for him.

"My buddy said you were looking for ballplayers, but I didn't believe him."

"Did he tell you that I struck out Babe Ruth?"

"Yeah," I said.

"That story seems to float around wherever I go, so if you're thinking that means I was a pretty good pitcher, forget it. A lot of pitchers struck out Babe Ruth. The other part of that story is that the last home run Babe Ruth ever hit as a Yankee he hit off of me when I was pitching for the Senators.

"But I don't have time to talk about me or Babe Ruth. I want to talk about you. I need some ballplayers. You're pretty good. Young, but I think you can learn. I lost players from last year's team. Some of them are playing in Mexico, so I came down here to get some Mexican players to play in the States. You're the only one in Cananea that could play for me, so don't ask about bringing along any of your buddies. I found out how much the mines are paying you. I can pay you that much while you're playing, plus I got the mines to say they will give you your job back when the season is over."

It sounded pretty good, and I did want to try playing baseball as a professional, but I had gotten used to that steady paycheck, and I didn't know whether to believe that the mining company would give me my job back.

Mr. Cohen was looking at me like he knew what I was thinking. "You want to play for the Bisbee-Douglas Copper Kings this season, be here at two o'clock next Sunday, and we'll go to Bisbee. I've got a couple of other guys who'll be going with us. Now all I have to do is find another pitcher."

"The best pitcher in Mexican baseball is already playing somewhere in *los Estados Unidos*. Maybe you can get him to play for you."

"Oh, yeah?" he said. "Who's that?"

"Chato Bello. He's my hero. I always wanted to pitch like him."

"Chato? You know Chato?"

"No, but I always wanted to."

"Then you have to come play for the Copper Kings, because that's where Chato Bello plays. He has been playing for me in the States for a couple of years."

That's all I needed to hear. I made up my mind on the spot. I was going to Bisbee, Arizona, to play for the Copper Kings for the 1952 season.

A week later Mr. Cohen showed up in an old battered Cadillac. He had a couple guys with him: Benjamin "Papalero" Valenzuela, a third baseman-outfielder from Hermosillo, and Arnulfo Manzo, a little left-handed pitcher he had picked off of one of the Mexican League clubs. We rode the fifty miles to Bisbee without saying much. When we got there, Mr. Cohen dropped Manzo and me off at a house where the people spoke Spanish and had agreed to have us stay with them for the season.

The next day Mr. Cohen sent a guy in a bus to pick us up and take us to the ballpark. They gave us our uniforms and lockers, and I dressed very quickly and got out on the field. I had been looking forward to meeting Chato Bello for a long time, and now I was just about to see him and talk to him. I looked across the infield and saw that there were some pitchers working out along the right field line. I walked up to one who looked like he was Mexican and introduced myself. He said his name was Oliverio Ortiz, but everybody called him "Baby."

I asked him where Chato Bello was.

"I've only been here a couple of days," he said. He pointed to a guy who was throwing to a catcher farther out in the field. "See that guy? His name is 'Blackie' Morales. He's been around here forever." I walked in the direction of the pitcher he had pointed out. "Hey, kid," he hollered after me. "My nickname is Baby, so don't let anybody start calling you that. OK?"

I pulled my cap down tight over my eyes and hoped it made me look a little older. When I reached Blackie Morales, I wasn't sure what to do. He was an older guy, and I didn't know if I could call him Blackie just like that. I sure didn't want to call him Mr. Morales.

He took a return throw from the catcher and tossed it up in the air and caught it behind his back then looked over at me. "Who are you?" he asked.

"Alberto Reyna."

"I'm Blackie Morales," he said, extending his hand. "What do they call you?"

"Beto is good," I answered.

"So what do you play?"

"Infield."

"Good. We need infielders. I wondered if you might be the pitcher Syd brought in, but I thought he was left-handed, and you're not," he said, looking at my glove.

"There's the pitcher," I said, pointing at Arnulfo Manzo, who was walking out toward the group. "Now, will you point out to me which pitcher is Chato Bello?"

"Chato," he said. "Why do you want to find Chato?"

"I know what a great pitcher he is. I saw him pitch in Mexico, and I know about the perfect game he pitched. He has always been my hero. When I was younger, I wanted to be a pitcher like him."

"Well, if you're looking for Chato, you've got to go to El Paso. He hasn't pitched here in a couple of years. I wish he was still here. He and I used to be the one-two punch, but he wanted to go somewhere else where he thought he had a better chance to get to the Big Leagues. Isn't happening there either, but you never know until you try."

"But Mister Cohen said he was pitching here. That's why I came."

Blackie shook his head and laughed. "When you ask him about it, he's gonna say that he doesn't always speak Spanish very good, and that he got the words mixed up. Syd went by the name of Pablo García when he was playing in Nogales, Sonora. He speaks Spanish better than I do. He must have wanted you pretty bad to tell you a story like that." Blackie was still laughing as I walked away.

We had a couple of practices before our season started. I was playing third base, shortstop, and second base. I think Mr. Cohen wanted to see if I could play the positions well enough to be a utility infielder. I was surprised when I found out Mr. Cohen was a player as well as a manager. He had to be over fifty years old, but he would take a turn out on the mound from time to time. Not much speed but a lot of motion and junk. His arm was gone, and he had learned to get by for an inning or two by keeping the hitters off balance.

Mr. Cohen was throwing batting practice the next day, and I was hitting ropes out to right field. I hit everything he threw, and I hit it hard. "OK, one more, *chamaco*. Let me see you hit this one." He threw a pitch that looked like a big balloon floating up there, but just as I swung, the bottom dropped out of it, and I almost fell down I missed it so bad. Francisco Bustamonte was working behind the plate, and he missed it too. The ball went bouncing to the backstop.

"What the hell was that, Syd?" he hollered to the mound.

"Knuckleball," Mr. Cohen said to his catcher. And then to me: "I bet your hero, Chato Bello, can't throw one of those."

His comment angered me because I thought he was putting Chato down. I walked out to the mound to talk to him, but I kept my voice in control, realizing it was the manager I was talking to. "Mr. Cohen, didn't you like Chato as a pitcher?"

"Chato was a very good pitcher," he said. "I wish he was still here."

"Then why did you tell me he was pitching here when he's not here anymore?"

"I'm sorry. I got the words mixed up. You know, Spanish isn't my native language, and sometimes I think I know it better than I do. I was trying to say he used to pitch here, and I probably made you think he still did. You want to meet Chato Bello? You will pretty soon. We start a home stand in a couple of days, then we go on the road to Phoenix, then

Tucson, and then El Paso where your hero is pitching. Can you wait that long?"

Mr. Cohen said exactly what Blackie said he would, but he also told me we played El Paso, and I didn't know that. After all those years of wanting to meet Chato Bello, I could wait a little longer. I would play the best ball I could for the Bisbee-Douglas Copper Kings and wait for our road trip that would take me to Chato.

When the season started, I was mostly on the bench, since there were players in the infield who were older and with more experience. But Mr. Cohen got me into games when he could. He used me as a pinch runner, and sometimes he put me in the game in the late innings when our team was ahead and once when we were way behind. I got a hit in that game and even stole second. It felt good to be out on the field with these older players.

Jimmy Cantú was my favorite player on the Copper Kings. He played left field and was a very good hitter. The guy who batted ahead of him was this big *gringo* who played first base named Van something or other. I could never remember his last name. When Van got a hit, the home town crowd always hollered, "Van can: Jimmy Cantú. Van can: Jimmy Cantú." I didn't know what it meant, but that hollering always got the crowd going. And when Jimmy Cantú got a hit, everybody went wild. It was really a lot of fun to play in front of a crowd like that. I always thought they were that way because they were mostly miners. Bisbee was a copper mining town, and since I worked as a miner in Cananea, I knew what kind of people they were: hard workers who enjoyed a night out with a few beers and a baseball game to take their mind off their hard lives in the mines. They loved it when Blackie pitched. He had been around there for a few years, and they felt like they knew him. He was a tough guy who would go out there and try to make the other team hit his best pitch.

They also loved Mr. Cohen. When he wasn't pitching, he coached third base. In between any action on the field, he would be talking to the people in the bleachers. He seemed to know a lot of them personally. They kidded him, and he always took it, but I could tell that as much as he played the funny man sometimes, he was all baseball. His head was in the game, and he hollered encouragement to the pitchers, positioned the outfielders and infielders, and gave signals to the batters.

When we weren't playing, the people in town all knew who we were and would come up and talk to us. I didn't know what they were saying, because I couldn't speak English, but a lot of them spoke Spanish, even some of the *gringos*, because this was a border town, and people grew up hearing the language. It was fun being a Copper King in Bisbee.

When we went on the road, it all changed. Wherever we went, the people hollered bad things at us and even said things about our families. Instead of talking to the people in the bleachers, Mr. Cohen was fighting with them, hollering back at them. Sometimes they threw things at him while he was coaching at third.

The travel was hard in other ways, too. We went on the old bus that picked us up for practice and home games. Pedro and Elias Osorio were the drivers. Most of the trips were long, and they took turns driving, so we could keep going. Since they didn't stop very much, there was a five-gallon can on the bus for us to piss in. Sometimes the smell from the can, and the heat, and the exhaust fumes made it hard to breathe. When the can got full or smelled too bad, the Osorio brother who was driving would pull off the road and someone (usually me because I was the youngest) would get the can off the bus and run out and dump it in the desert, and we would be off again.

Mr. Cohen never came on the bus with us. He drove his old Cadillac, and we would see him behind us or sometimes in front. There were times that he would just disappear, and we wouldn't see him until we got to the ballpark.

After we played in Tucson and Phoenix, we headed for El Paso. This was a very long trip, and I was getting tired of riding on the smelly bus. I tried to sleep, but it was too hot. I was moving around looking for a cooler place when Blackie said to me, "Hey, *chamaco*, sit down." He moved over in his seat so I could sit. Blackie had taken up calling me *chamaco* like Mr. Cohen did. "How long have you been chasing Chato now?"

"I saw him pitch in 1948," I answered. "So that's four years."

"What are you going to say to Chato when you see him?"

"I just want to meet him and talk to him about the perfect game he pitched in 1946. My father doesn't believe he really did it. He says the gamblers set that up, so I just want to talk to him about it."

"I don't know when he's going to pitch against us, but you can bet he will. I'll give you some advice: When Chato's pitching, don't try to talk to him before the game. He likes to get his game face on. Get his mind ready to pitch. So leave him alone. After the game—especially if he wins—is when you want to tell him who you are and talk to him."

I thanked Blackie for the advice. As it turned out, Chato was set to pitch on opening night of our three-game series. And that just happened to be my first start of the season. Mr. Cohen played me at second base and batted me eighth. What a thrill. My first start as a professional baseball player, and Chato Bello, the only man to ever pitch a perfect game in Mexico, was the starting pitcher. I knew this game was something I would never forget. When Chato came out of the dugout to warm up, I saw that Blackie didn't follow his own advice. He had been shagging flies in the outfield, and he moved over to the side and stopped Chato. The two talked for a couple of minutes. Then Chato started his warm-up.

I was following Jimmy Cantú in the lineup, and Jimmy got the first hit of the night against Chato, a ringing double into the left field gap. Jimmy stood on second base clapping his hands, and I started thinking that if I could follow with a single, I'd have my first RBI. I was excited about the possibility. As I stood in the batter's box ready for the first pitch, Chato wheeled and threw to the shortstop, who had moved in behind the base runner, and Jimmy Cantú got picked off second base. In baseball, even veteran players like Jimmy were made to look silly from time to time, especially by a good pitcher like Chato.

I'd lost my chance for an RBI, but I still wanted to hit the ball hard into the gap in right field, especially since the defense was set up for me to pull the ball to left. Chato started in for the sign and came set for the first pitch. The ball was on the way, and I saw in a flash that it was aimed right for my head. I flopped hard and fast onto my stomach. I picked myself up and stared out at Chato as I got back into the batter's box. Chato wasted no time throwing his next pitch, this one not at my head, but it hit me hard in the ribs. I didn't let it show that it hurt as I tossed my bat toward the dugout and trotted toward first base. "Hey, *chamaco*," Chato hollered at me on the way, "Tell your old man he don't know what he's talking about."

So Blackie and Chato were still pretty good friends I realized, since Blackie had told Chato what my father has said about the gamblers. I could understand why Chato had gotten upset. He didn't like anyone doubting that his accomplishment of pitching a perfect game was anything less than his talent.

Chato struck out Jesús Santos, our pitcher, on three strikes right down the middle of the plate. I studied Chato as he pitched and thought with that big leg kick of his that I could get a good jump. I took off on his first pitch to our leadoff man and stole second base. The catcher's throw wasn't even close. Chato turned around and glared at me. I was not making a friend out of my hero. My extra effort made no difference as I died on second when Nicholas Cappelli struck out.

Chato had his way with our team for the next three innings, giving up only a scratch single. When it was my turn to bat again in the sixth inning, I didn't know what to expect. I found out quickly as Chato knocked me down again. I stood up and dug my cleats in harder, and Chato knocked me down again. When I stood up this time, I didn't dig in so hard, and Chato quickly threw three strikes past me, all on the outside corner. I swung weakly at the last one. As I got back in the dugout, Mr. Cohen said to me, "Looks like Chato doesn't like you, *chamaco.*"

I didn't get my last at bat against Chato. We were losing 2–0 in the ninth inning, and Mr. Cohen had Bosco Verbica pinch hit for me. My first game had ended with no hits to my credit. The front of my uniform was filthy from me flopping in the dirt to get away from Chato's knockdown pitches, but the seat was dirty too from my stolen base. At least I had that to remember my first start as a professional baseball player.

We only won one of the games against El Paso—the last one, but that made the trip home seem a little shorter. The team was happy to get off the road, and after a day off, we would start another long home stand. I didn't know anything about our schedule; I just showed up at the ballpark when I was told. After we played a series against Juarez, I found out El Paso was coming to town. Surely Chato would pitch one of the games, and I might get another chance to hit against him.

I wasn't in the lineup when Chato started the middle game of the series, and I hadn't expected that I would be, but

I got into the game at second base in the fourth inning when Ed Serrano hurt his knee legging out an infield hit. I pinch ran for him and went to third when Van whatever his name was followed with another single. Now it was Jimmy Cantú's turn, and the crowd started their chant: "Van can; Jimmy Cantú. Van can; Jimmy Cantú." Jimmy came through with another hit, and I scored easily. The crowd was going wild, but mine was the only run scored that inning. We had been down by four runs, but we started feeling that we might have Chato on the run.

We got another run in the fifth, and I made an outstanding play in the sixth with a leaping catch that robbed one of their hitters and led to another being doubled off of second. When I came to bat in our half of the sixth, I got a big hand from the Bisbee fans. I was determined to get something going. I dug in and glared out at Chato, almost daring him to hit me. He didn't knock me down but pitched me tight inside. The second pitch was in the same place, but I held my ground. He had two balls on me now, but if he thought he had me set up like the last time I batted against him, he would try to get me to chase a pitch outside. He did, and I hit the ball where it was pitched, and it went sailing into right field, just where Mr. Cohen would want me to hit it.

When I rounded first base and came back to stand on the bag, a shiver ran through me as the crowd roared. I looked at Chato on the pitcher's mound. He had a little smile on his face and gave me a nod. Then he turned to pitch to Van whatever his name was. I took a lead off first and watched

Chato get ready to deliver his pitch, and then, all of a sudden, he whirled and threw to the first baseman, who quickly tagged me. Chato had picked me off. I stood and looked at him, and he wagged a finger at me and gave me a big smile.

I turned and trotted back to the dugout. With everybody looking at me, it seemed like the longest run I ever made. Mr. Cohen yanked his cap from his head and threw it down on the dugout floor and began stomping on it. I came down the steps and went to the other side of the dugout and sat by myself. Van hit a home run, and all of a sudden, it seemed like we were back in the game. The crowd started their chant: "Van can; Jimmy Cantú. Van can; Jimmy Cantú."

I stood up and walked to the edge of the dugout to watch Jimmy Cantú bat. As bad as my mistake had been, I knew I would get over it. I would forget about it. The only thing I would remember and tell my children—and hopefully my grandchildren—is that I got a hit off of Chato Bello, the first player in the history of Mexican baseball to pitch a perfect game.

Recollections of a High School Benchwarmer

by Daniel Romo

AKE ME OUT TO THE BALLGAME. TAKE ME OUT with the crowd.

No one came to watch us play. Bleachers of tiered emptiness. Our game lacked the allure of long limbs stretching at maximum capacity soaring to score a basket. Or Friday night drums in between first downs serving as the heartbeat of the school. It was simple. "You catch the ball, you throw the ball, you hit the ball," words our coach instilled in us. The only time we got nervous was when our fathers came to watch us play, only to find their sons watching other fathers' children playing.

Buy me some peanuts and cracker jacks. I don't care if I never get back.

We spit sunflower seeds with first-string elegance, shells pelting gum wrappers on the ground with pinpoint precision. And we lined up empty Gatorade bottles when the coach wasn't looking. They were glass back then. We became better at makeshift bowling than actual baseball. Each flick of the wrist akin to a pitch. Bottles crashing to the ground like hit batsmen. And if one of us ever got the call to replace a starter, our dugout game was halted—boys that bonded over lack of playing time. Seven innings marked the end of the games. We usually worked in five frames.

Let me root, root, root for the home team. If they don't win it's a shame.

I didn't care whether we won or lost. I just wanted to witness a good game. Maybe because I was bitter my playing time was relegated to mop up. My only action: chasing foul balls hit over the backstop. But I felt no guilt for my apathy. *It's not about winning or losing but how you play the game* is not applicable to second-stringers.

For it's one, two, three strikes you're out

Sometimes I drive by the old ball field on my way home from buying milk, bacon, butter, or other domesticated staples that come with being a father. It no longer hurts. The feeling of selling myself short. Of fanning former insecure flames sparking *what could have been*. I'm content to write about my near misses. Misses like looking at a third strike. Like a slow grounder between the legs. Like a fly ball scraping the edge of center fielder's glove, almost robbing the cleanup hitter of a home run, but falling over the fence... just out of reach.

at the old, ball, game…

Down the Line

by Edward Vidaurre

SWINGING AT BRUISED LEATHER BASEBALLS AND TRYING to keep it between second and third base. Barrio rules. We were latch-key kids living near four miles south of Dodger Stadium, or, as the older *veteranos* in the neighborhood called it, Chavez Ravine. They claim the *gobierno* came down on the landowners who were Mexican-American and took their *pedazo* of the American Dream. Why? I don't know, but it never stopped them from wearing blue-and-white *"doyer"* caps and being proud when "Fernandomania" took the baseball world by storm.

You already knew who would win, who would hope to win, and who would struggle. Chepito would struggle most. He bent and hunched over the plate and always swung late, making sure the ball would go foul or down the line in the wrong direction. These were the rules plain and simple. For Chepito the game was hard and complicated. Then there was Juan, square-jawed, muscular: *el mero mero honronero*. His brothers were all athletes—even his beautiful sister, María could outrun us. We would all pause and wait to see how far he could hit the ball. All the *chavalitos* would run past the center-fielder—back, back, back where it would be gone.

The bully gang-bangers rode around in "borrowed" bicycles with cigarettes hanging from their lips as the stillness of summer allowed for an inch of ash to hang from their pubescent hairline mustaches. The girls sat at a distance while the boys glanced over, trying to hit the ball into the gap at left-center, showing off, yelling loudly with their off-key mini machismo selves. I sat watching the homies making memories in my mind, sipping on a cream soda until it was my turn to bat. We played hard and tattooed sweat marks on our t-shirts, making spider web designs across our backs. Some of us had plastic gloves with half our hands sticking out and some had the leather mitts that were passed down from their older siblings with spit stains, and—if they were lucky— a Steve Garvey autograph.

If you hit the ball between right-center it would carry towards the cafeteria of the school grounds where we played after the last employee left for the day. Not too far from where I tasted my first kiss from Chicana lips, moist and strange—her tongue confused me into manhood, making me *firme* after rounding second with the prettiest girl I knew.

Down the line, down the streets, *curvas* thrown at us— life always trying to count us out. We played until the first call from our mothers rang through the barrio, until the sun abandoned us, until the gunshots sounded, or until Vin Scully's voice was turned down on the television to listen to the radio broadcast of Jaime Jarrín's voice translating the game known to us as *béisbol*.

One Inning at a Time till Nine

by René Saldaña, Jr.

First Pitch

Rudy slaps the ball
Into the leather cave
Of my worn mitt.
"You good?" he wants to know.
I scratch at the ground
At the foot of the mound
With the toe of my cleats.
"I'm good," I say.
"Really? Cuz you don't look it,"
He says. "You good, yeah?"
When I don't say,
He says, "Three up three down, then."
I grab the ball and slap it back
Into my glove: "One inning
At a time til nine," I say.
"It'll all be fine." Our ritual
Before every game, but today

They're just words. "Okay, then,"
He says and heads
To his crouch behind the plate.
"Play ball!" goes the ump.
The batter struts to his place
In the box outlined in white,
Cocksure, tapping the plate
With his bat, a snort,
A homerun in his eyes.
I circle the mound,
Kneading the ball,
Then climb to the rubber.
I toe it, too, and wonder
If mom's okay at home.
The ump grunts from his crouch,
"Batter up."
Rudy calls for the heat
To open with. Up and in.
I nod, and I deliver.
I hear my dad in the stands:
"Hey, batta batta batta,
"Swing!" Which he does:
Strike one.
With mom bad as she is
I have to wonder how Dad's smiling.
"Hey, batta, batta, swing!"

Batter Up

Ruben from Abram's up,
Abram, the town down a ways from us.
Ruben casts a big shadow
Over the plate,
And though at school
We run in the same circles,
Today, we're rivals.
I'm looking to strike him out,
He's looking to knock me off the mound
With a shot right at my head
If he can manage it,
Or to knock the wind out of me
With a shot over the fence.
I've got him at
2 balls, 2 strikes, fouled off a couple more.
But I'm bound and determined
And nothing he can do
To knock me down further than I already am.
I'm here playing this game
While mom's home wearing
The saddest look in the whole wide world.
"Come on, *mi'jo*," I hear my dad say
From the otherwise stingy crowd.
"Hard and fast," he says.
Rudy calls for a curve.
I shake my head no.

His pointer finger rigid this time,
He slaps it against the inside of his thigh,
Insisting.
He knows the hitters better than me,
But my dad's calling what I want to throw,
So I shake my head no,
Tap the rubber twice to let him know
It's coming down the middle,
Hard and fast.
A swing, a miss,
And my heart back to normal,
Except that my mom's still home
Taking her own cuts at
Harder and faster pitches
Than I could ever chuck.
And me and my dad
Here instead of there,
With her.

Two on, Two out

Top of the fourth now,
With a score of 2-0,
Our lead.
I've struck out four,
Given away a walk, and just the one hit.
So, man on first, man on second.
My heart's beating hard.

I check my man on second,
Who's taking a careful lead,
Nothing much to worry over.
It's the guy at the plate's
Got my nerves shook.
The count's 3 and 2,
And for the first time
This whole game
I feel doubt creeping in.
It's way away yet,
On the outskirts of the field of play,
But the shadow's certainly there,
At the edges of my brain.
I pull off the rubber,
The ump steps off the catcher's back,
The batter, though, he stays rooted,
His eyes square on me,
To intimidate me,
To show me up,
But what do I care?
I talk secrets into my mitt, then
Climb back onto the mound,
Sneak a look over my shoulder
To spot the shadows creeping,
But there isn't anything there.
In my head I see the next pitch play out:
There's the crack of the bat, a line drive
To short, who dives to snag that ball.
He leaps to his feet and in that split second

Knows to throw to first is the way to go.
In the here and now,
My batter's swinging no matter what.
Pumped with the vision, I toss
The ball hard and down the middle,
Just above the knees.
He's got to know it's coming.
It's my go-to pitch.
When I look back up,
As the ball is flying away from me
The batter sees it pushing in
Toward him, and the same fear
I was feeling a few moments back
He's feeling now,
And that's when I realize something big,
Bigger than getting this guy out,
Bigger than this game even,
Bigger than the game period,
That for this one pitch, at least,
I hadn't thought about my mom.
The batter takes the best cut he's got,
But he misses, and I get us out of the tight jam
I'd put us in. Behind me, I feel
The team's sigh, deep, warm,
And how it's blowing away
The shadow, that is,
Until my next time on the mound.

The Seventh-Inning Stretch

Which is so not like in the Majors
Where they take an extended
Commercial break and the crowd sings
"Take Me Out to the Ballpark."
Here, when we strike them out,
Tag them clean at second,
Snag that fly ball out the sky,
We run off the field, they go on.
We take a seat, those of us
Who've still got to wait
Our turn,
Or shove our helmets
Onto our heads if we're next in line:
One at the plate,
Another on deck, shadow-swinging,
A third, in the hole,
Fingers clutching the chain link fence.
I'm the one next after him.
My helmet next to me on the bench,
I can hear myself breathing,
Wondering if I'll have my turn
This go-round, or will I have to wait
Till the bottom of the eighth?
I get my answer quick
When Zamorita connects for a double.
I take my spot at the fence,

And wonder now,
How my mom is doing.
She just found out today
She's got cancer,
And told me and my dad
She needed some time alone,
For us to go to the game and do
The best I could, to give her
That much. She'll be alright, she said.
Looking through the fence
Beyond this field, beyond those trees,
Beyond my sight,
I know she's home
Crying, or all cried out by now,
Likely sitting with the family photo bucket
On her lap revisiting times
When there was no great shadow looming,
When life lay ahead of her, of us
Long and pretty like a homerun
Ball hit toward center field,
The kind the batter knows
Will clear the fence easy
The moment the bat connects.
He feels it in his hands, his wrists,
Up his elbows, to his shoulders.
He can see it land beyond the fence
Before it even takes flight.
It's electric, that moment, in your gut.
But now life's not like that.

Not for my mother. Not for my dad.
And not for me.
It's darker at our edges,
No silver lining to speak of.
And I'm up to bat now,
Zamorita at third, Junior on first,
One out. I'll take my cuts,
One, two, three,
And hope I can deliver.
Which I don't. I strike out
Just like that.
Not the least electrifying.

Top of the Ninth

I've pitched a decent game,
Let one run in.
Abram's down to their last out,
And wouldn't you know it,
It's Ruben at the plate.
Still a tower, still that stare,
Wanting to either knock it or me out.
One good swing'll do it.
But one good pitch will finish it, too.
A ball and 2 strikes.
Rudy calls a curve,
My dad the fire,
But man, my arm is dying out here,

I don't know if I've got it no more,
Not even for one last hard and fast.
Rudy reminds me he wants his curve.
Ruben probably knows it'll be a curve.
My dad knows it'll be a curve.
But he wants the heat.
I'd rather be at home than on this mound
Checking to make sure the runner on second,
The tying run, is leading close to the bag or loose.
But I'd rather be at home than on this mound.
I tell myself he's nothing to worry over,
Let him fly if he will.
I'd rather be at home than on this mound.
Ruben, the go-ahead run, is anxious
To make his play,
And I'd rather be at home than on this mound.
I wind up, rear up high, and let go
The hardest, fastest pitch I got left in me.
It happens to be enough for a swing and a miss.
We've won the game,
And the bench clears
And the guys behind me run in
And the coaches jump for joy
And my dad in the crowd is quiet now,
Crying, I can see, for me, but more for Mom,
And I run as hard and as fast as I can off this field and
Beyond the fence, beyond those trees, down those streets
Back home, to my mother, where I want to be.
Where I need to be.

Ritualidades: Rituals

by Juan Antonio González

AL HACER UN GESTO CON LA NARIZ PORQUE algo le molestaba, se dio cuenta cuán desagradable es el olor a tabaco encendido. No lo aguantaba; esto ocurre a menudo con quien deja de fumar. Al desintoxicarse la nariz, se da uno cuenta de la paciencia que debieron ejercer los amigos, sobre todo aquéllos que no fumaban, y se aprecia su benevolencia al aguantar el olor del tabaco durante y después del consumo. De este apego a la amistad se dio cuenta el 6 de octubre de 1981, y desde entonces fue mayor su consideración. No, no había sido la fecha en la que había dejado de fumar, sino aquélla en la que se percató de la insolencia de quiénes ejercían su derecho tan indistinta e indiscriminadamente que no les importaba si estaban en sitio cerrado o rodeados de personas que no apreciaban el hábito, y menos el olor.

Había ocurrido en un viernes de otoño. Recuerda los rituales: ponerse una chaqueta rompe vientos, y hacer otro tanto con los niños antes de salir. La idea era llegar temprano; habría regalos para los primeros en acudir a la

**FTER SCRUNCHING UP HIS NOSE AT THE BOTH-**
ersome smell, he realized just how nasty
burning tobacco is. He couldn't stomach it,
as is often the case with people who quit
smoking. Once your nose has been
disintoxicated, you understand the patience
your friends, especially those who don't smoke, have shown
you, and you learn to appreciate their goodwill in putting up
with the stink that you would exhale, that would cling to your
clothes. He learned of this loyalty of his friends on October 6,
1981, and afterwards he became more considerate. No, that
wasn't the date he stopped smoking: it was the moment he
noticed the insolence of people who exercised their right to
smoke in such a broad, indiscriminate way that it didn't
matter to them whether they were in a closed space or
surrounded by people with no liking of the habit, much less
the smell.

It had happened one Friday in the fall. He remembers
the rituals: slip into a windbreaker, get the kids ready to go.
The idea was to get there early—they gave out prizes to the

cita. También disfrutaría de sentarse a sus anchas y curiosear con toda la información disponible: asistir al Astrodome era la experiencia más maravillosa de la vida, máxime cuando tendrían de rivales a los Dodgers de los Ángeles en postemporada, y que el duelo de lanzadores sería entre Fernando Valenzuela por éstos últimos, y Nolan Ryan por los locales. Por eso, llevar a los niños –el mayor de cuatro y el menor de dos años– sentía que era una etapa ineludible e inaplazable: un ritual de paso. El aprecio del "rey de los deportes" se daba así, estrechando lazos familiares en un compromiso indestructible. Así se había iniciado él: con las peregrinaciones hacia la ciudad vecina, que tenía equipo de liga AA, debido a la inclinación de su padre por el deporte.

Arrellanado en su sitio, se le ocurrió pedir una *lait* para no desentonar; entonces no le gustaban las cervezas oscuras. Le echó ojo al vecino que estaba disfrutando de un *hot dog* de medio metro, y relleno de un menjunje oscuro que debía ser chile con carne y queso amarillo que olía bien. Sondeó a los hijos sobre sus preferencias, y les compró palomitas y refrescos, mientras obtuvo una torta de salchicha descomunal. ¡Qué importaba si se llenaba de salsa la chaqueta: la llevaría al *cleaners* a su regreso y ya.

Había decidido llevar las estadísticas; compró la revista semanal que indicaba quiénes formarían parte del encuentro. Repasó los nombres de jardineros y cuadro base; leyó el porcentaje de bateo del receptor, y los porcentajes de carreras limpias de los lanzadores abridores y relevistas, incluyendo al *taponero* estrella: Se hizo una nota mental para apreciar cómo le lanzaría Nolan Ryan a Pedro Guerrero,

first ones to show up. He also enjoyed sprawling in his seat and thumbing through all the available information: going to the Astrodome was the most wonderful experience in life, especially when the post-season rivals were the Dodgers and the duel would be between their Fernando Valenzuela and Nolan Ryan of the Astros. That's why bringing the boys—the older four, the younger two—felt like an unavoidable phase that could not be postponed: a rite of passage. This was how you acquired an appreciation for the "king of sports," strengthening family ties in an indestructible commitment. He had started the same way, accompanying his baseball-inclined father on pilgrimages to a neighboring city that had a Double-A minor league team.

Settling into his seat, he decided to order a light beer to fit in better; at the time, he didn't like the heavier brews. He glanced over at a neighbor who was enjoying a foot-long hot dog slathered in some dark, delicious-smelling mess that appeared to be chili and cheese. He checked with the boys as to their preference and then bought them popcorn and soda, getting himself a huge brat on a bun. Who cared if he dripped stuff all over his jacket? He'd just take it to the cleaners when they got back, and problem solved.

He wanted to keep the stats and score, so he picked up a copy of the weekly magazine that broke down the roster of each team. He went over the names of the outfielders and basemen; he read the batting average of the catcher and ERA rates of starting pitchers and relievers, including the star closer. He made a mental note to study how Nolan Ryan

terror de todos los lanzadores por su exagerado poder para conectar la bola recta.

Pero a medida que se acercaba el inicio del encuentro fueron llegando más y más aficionados. Las tribunas, a esas alturas, estaban eufóricas por la algarabía de sus ocupantes. El "rey de los deportes", en su generosidad, esparcía buenas relaciones inter familiares. Todo mundo participaba de la euforia: el equipo local con su lanzador estrella, contra el equipo rival, con su "fenómeno de lanzar" en el montículo. Nolan contra Fernando, o al revés, dependiendo cuál fuera el favorito.

Se escuchó la voz de *pléibol*, y los equipos que habían estado haciendo ejercicios de calentamiento se aprestaron a dar inicio a la jornada. Como equipo visitante, Dodgers inició el ataque. De los primeros tres bateadores que se acercaron al plato, dos fueron *ponchados*. Entre los lanzamientos rectos de 97 ó 98 millas por hora, de repente aparecía una curva *venenosa* a 78. Parecía que se iban de boca los bateadores intentando alcanzarla antes de tiempo. Y es que se debía preparar el *bat* y dar el *swing* a tiempo para alcanzar la bola rápida y cuando venía el cambio de velocidad, el bateador se veía mal, como si fuera novato. Sin embargo, no temían al ridículo ya que enfrentar a Nolan Ryan era hacer cita con el *ponche*.

Salió a cerrar la entrada Fernando y de los altavoces, precediendo su ingreso, se escuchó la canción de ABBA del mismo nombre que el público vitoreó: tanta era su popularidad en todas partes, pero sobre todo entre los latinoamericanos aficionados del béisbol, y en Texas siempre

would pitch to Pedro Guerrero, feared by pitchers for his incredible power to slug fast balls.

As start time for the showdown approached, more and more fans arrived. The stands, at this point, thrummed euphorically with the excited clamor of the crowd. The "king of sports," in its generosity, built up the bonds between family and friends. Everyone shared in the excitement: the local team with its ace pitcher against the visitors and their "pitching phenomenon" on the mound. It was basically Nolan against Fernando, or vice versa, depending on your favorite.

The shout of *play ball* went up, and the two teams, which had been warming up, took to the field to get the game started. As visiting team, the Dodgers began the attack. Of the first three batters that approached the plate, two were struck out. Among the 97- or 98-mph fast balls, a nasty 78-mph curve ball would sling its way through the air. The batters nearly threw themselves on their faces trying to connect before the ball was in the strike zone. Of course, repeatedly getting the bat ready and trying to swing in time to smack those fast balls left a batter unprepared for the change in speed and made him look bad, like a rookie. But none of them were worried about being ridiculed—facing Nolan Ryan was like having a date with the Whiff.

Fernando came out to close the inning. From the speakers, just before his entrance, blared the song by ABBA that bore the same name the crowd now shouted again and again: that's how popular he was, everywhere, but especially among Latino fans of baseball. In Texas they were legion.

ha habido muchos. Se enfrentó a los tres primeros bateadores y los dominó con su lanzamiento de tirabuzón (*scrúbol*). Desde su posición zurda en el montículo, Fernando alzaba los ojos al cielo para pedir inspiración, y soltaba unos lanzamientos que eludían el *swing* del bateador.

Después de la primera entrada el público se percató que el duelo anticipado rebasaría todas las expectativas y nos aprestamos para disfrutar del encuentro.

Casi 30 años han pasado y aún recuerdo la anotación final. Ganó Ryan y perdió Valenzuela por 3 a 1. Recuerdo los rituales familiares antes, durante y posteriores al encuentro. Todos salimos con gorras nuevas del estadio, por cortesía de una de las grandes cadenas comerciales. (Aún conservo la mía.) Sin embargo, no fue lo esperado del duelo de lanzadores, que por cierto fue magnífico y rebasó todas las expectativas, lo que me regresa al sitio, a pesar de la distancia física y temporal, sino haber tenido que aguantar a un aficionado, de avanzada edad, que sentado en la fila anterior disfrutó del encuentro dándole chupadas a su puro. Cuando uno fue fumador y deja el vicio, se agudiza el sentido del olfato.

De manera que ahora, el viento a distancia en un espacio abierto, me retorna al pasatiempo familiar, al ritual de familia, al Astrodome, ahora ya en obsolescencia para justas beisbolísticas, que devana el pasaje de las horas para situarse de nuevo en aquel 6 de octubre de 1981.

He went up against the first three batters, dominating them with his screwball. From his leftie stance there on the mound, Fernando cast his eyes toward heaven for inspiration, then he hurled amazing pitches that slipped past each batter's swing.

After that first inning, the crowd understood that this duel would shatter every expectation. We prepared to revel in the showdown.

Almost thirty years have passed, and I still remember that final score. Ryan won and Valenzuela lost, 3 to 1. I recall the familiar rituals before, during, and after the game. We all left the stadium with new caps thanks to some massive chain store (I still have mine). But it isn't that highly anticipated pitching duel—clearly magnificent and historical—that brings me back to that place, despite its distance in space and time, but the fact that I had to put up with an elderly fan who, sitting in the row behind us, spent the entire game sucking on a cigar. As someone who was a smoker but managed to quit, my sense of smell had become very keen.

So now, the wind blowing the stench of tobacco to me from some distant point, I am drawn back to that family pastime, to that ritual of fathers and sons, to the Astrodome—now closed to the jousting of sluggers and pitchers—as the hours unspool till I find myself again in the stands on that 6th of October, 1981...

—Translated by David Bowles

Baseball over the Moon

by Kathryn Lane

I CALLED MY FATHER *CORQUE,* A NAME I CHRISTENED HIM with when I started talking, imitating the sound I heard when the ranch hands addressed him as Don Jorge. He longed so much for a son, the dream of every cattleman in Northern Mexico, that he took me along with him when he worked the ranch, teaching me to ride a horse on my own by my third birthday, and training me to round up cattle, side by side with the cowboys, by my fifth year.

"When you run after a stray cow, give a little slack to the reins and let the horse do the work," I remember him instructing me.

For my sixth birthday he gave me a big, beautiful palomino that I named Vago, a horse that meant as much to me as a dog might mean to most kids my age. By my eighth birthday, I could handle Vago very well. At least that's what the cowboys would tell my father. "She still has a lot to learn," he would respond.

At night, after Corque and I spent hard days working in the corrals, my parents enjoyed time together in the comfort of the living room. I could overhear my mother coax him, as she sat at one end of the sofa massaging Corque's tired feet while he lay sprawled out over the sofa, "You need to let her choose her own activities, like playing with dolls. She will never become a feminine little girl if you insist on raising her like a boy."

"Very well then: it's time to try again to have a son," he always replied. With that remark, he had the habit of leading my mother to the bedroom, regardless of the time of day.

Life seemed good to me without siblings to share it with. Carlos, the foreman's son, had four sisters and he fought with them all the time, and the four girls fought amongst themselves, too. I felt lucky to be an only child. Most of the time, I loved the attention I received, but there were times when Corque did not like how I behaved and would punish me, letting me cry until he tired of my whimpering. Then he would yell. "That's enough, Nati: cut it out."

Corque played baseball with me, teaching me the subtleties of the game, at least as many as any eight year old could understand. He bought the best mitts, balls and bats. On the back side of the house, a short distance from the large window where he watched from his comfortable chair in the breakfast nook, he'd built a mound and behind home plate, closer to the kitchen window, a wire net on two tall poles to catch the balls. When the foreman, Don Cuco, had free time, he pitched for me, with his son, the twelve year old Carlos, assigned to the catcher's box.

As I stood next to home plate hitting the balls Don Cuco pitched, I knew that Corque, relaxing from the hard ranch work, watched from the breakfast nook, sipping a shot of tequila. If I made a big mistake, the kitchen door would fly open and he would shout instructions, just as a coach might yell from the dugout: "Don't swing unless it's a strike!"

On Sunday afternoons, Corque joined us for baseball practice. I was less intimidated by Corque's coaching when he left the house to join us on the field. Anticipating his outbursts over my mistakes as he stood close by made it easier for me not to be embarrassed in front of Carlos.

"Make a smooth, controlled swing with the bat," he commanded. "Keep your eye on Don Cuco as he pitches the ball, watch the ball, watch the ball! Now swing!" And the ball would usually sail past my swinging bat straight into Carlos's mitt.

"Now let's work on your stance," Corque would tell me. "Feet a bit more than shoulder width apart. Your feet need to be right here to start with, just this far from home plate. Try to remember that."

He also adjusted the middle knuckles on each hand so they lined up on the bat. "This helps in executing the proper swing." He would state it as if he were talking to someone who really did know how to hit the ball.

"Okay, *Cuco, pichea otra vez*," Corque said. And Don Cuco prepared for the next pitch.

"If the pitch is not a strike, then don't swing," he reminded me.

As Corque worked with me, Don Cuco waited patiently at the mound for the next command, but Carlos quickly became bored. At these times, Carlos would rub the glove against his face as if to compare its leather to the rawhide processed on the ranch. The rawhide was used for stretching over bed frames to serve as the support for thin feather mattresses used in the bunkhouse where the seasonal ranch hands slept. Don Cuco cut the rawhide into long strips, soaked them in salt water to prepare them to be woven into a tight over and under pattern on the bed frames. Carlos, always helpful, sat at his father's side, pulling the long, thin strips from the tub of salted water, testing each one for malleability. The strips that remained too stiff were thrown back into the tub for additional soaking.

When Carlos's turn came up at the batter's box, he cast aside the mitt and boredom. His face lit up like a Christmas tree as he walked up to take the bat, standing tall in front of his own dad, who had moved to the catcher's position.

Taking the bat from Carlos, Corque demonstrated how to position it. "Place the bat behind your back, like this, gripping it with both hands, right elbow up in the air keeping the barrel facing the catcher. Then swing the bat through like a machete cutting pampas grass at mid-stalk."

After Carlos had practiced a few warm-up swings, Corque would stop pitching long enough to explain hip rotations. "Now show me how you're going to hit a good ball coming towards you. Remember the back hip should drive the rotation."

"Si, *Patrón*," Carlos said, respectfully referring to my father as the boss. On cue Carlos would take his normal coil, stride, and then rotate his hips open while Corque continued commenting on Carlos's positioning.

"Hips should rotate on a level plane, like this," my father said. Corque used his hands to demonstrate an imaginary plane within which Carlos's hips should move. "Your back foot should pivot for a smooth rotation. Don't lean forward over the plate, or you'll lose your balance."

Once satisfied that Carlos understood, my Corque pitched the ball to the twelve year-old, who could hit the ball and send it way out into the yard, even as far away as the chicken coop at times. On really good hits, he smacked the ball all the way to the bunkhouse, as if trying to bounce the ball off the rawhide strips of the bed frames he helped construct.

On good hits, when the ball flew beyond the playing field, instead of waiting for me to retrieve the ball, Don Cuco would throw another one to my father from the stash he carried in his jacket. At these times, Carlos, his chest pumped up, would stand a few seconds looking like he owned the world, staring at me as if expecting me to break into applause. Don Cuco watched with growing satisfaction as his son's swing improved. The individual coaching lasted for a short period, only long enough for Corque to show his appreciation to the father and son for their patience in working with me throughout the week.

For Carlos, being batter was the highlight of his existence. At school he stood three inches taller when he bragged, "*El Patrón* pitched me a ball that I cracked straight over the moon." Some of his classmates did not believe Carlos actually played *béisbol* with *el Patrón* while other boys sniveled with envy.

During the spring and early summer, when the seasonal workers arrived, we formed two teams. I had my own little mitt and played outfielder. I still remember the big smile on Corque's face the day I surprised him with my first circus catch as I dived like an acrobat after the ball and came back up with it in my mitt.

At the end of every summer, when the heavy seasonal work ended, we traveled, like all Mexican families who could afford it, from the ranch to the border town of El Paso to shop. Without air-conditioning in the car, Corque always had us on the road by 4:00 am to take advantage of the cooler morning hours. The extended family crammed into the old Buick: my grandmother Natalia, the one I'd been named after and who I called Tita; Carmen, the nanny; and Negro, the Labrador.

Then the gifts for my grandmother's sister, *la tía abuela*, and her family who offered us their home during our stays in El Paso, would be brought out and stacked next to the car, gifts that took organized effort to prepare. Two days prior to the trip, my mother would call all female hands to the kitchen to make tender, succulent tamales, first soaking the corn kernels in lime water, rinsing and grinding them into fine cornmeal, next preparing the chili, mixing it with other aromatic spices and cooking it with the meats, and on the final day before the trip, adding lard and chicken broth to the cornmeal and beating it by hand for hours until a spoonful of *masa* floated in a glass of water. The assembly line of women, my mother, Tita, Carmen and I spread the *masa* and pork or chicken fillings on the softened corn husks, steamed them to perfection and cooled them before packing them in a large clay pot, covering the top with brown paper held in place by a large rubber band to keep Negro from eating the tamales, complete with husks, as he had on last year's trip. Baskets of freshly cut apples and peaches from the orchard, jars of homemade jam, a box with my favorite dessert, sticky slabs of *cajeta de membrillo* wrapped in waxed paper and the pot of tamales were finally loaded in every nook of space left in the trunk next to our suitcases, stacked on the floor inside the car and shoved into slivers of space on the car seats between the passengers in the already crowded Buick.

The dirt road from the ranch and the narrow asphalted highway that started in San Buenaventura took the scenic route, my father always liked to tell visitors, when explaining that the road serpentined its way throughout *el norte* before finally hitting the Pan-American Highway and turning north to the border. The road trip, five hours of tortuous driving in the hot Chihuahua desert, opened my imagination to the possibility of errant knights on horseback attacking our gray and white Buick, or herds of elephants crossing our path, bellowing their pleasure at finding a waterhole. I kept those fantasies to myself but asked my parents and Tita endless questions about the terrain, the mountains in the distance, the deer, coyotes, skunks, snakes, prairie dogs or other wildlife that appeared along the road.

Every year, part of the ritual after a couple of hours of my endless chattering, my mother paid me to keep quiet, money that I inevitably spent on baseball caps and giant jaw cracking gum balls. We usually stayed at *tía abuela*'s for ten days, shopping, eating in fancy restaurants, taking my Tita and her sister to the bull fights in Ciudad Juarez on Sunday afternoon, and seeing movies almost every day, the big epics with gladiators or the biblical ones with casts of thousands, to make up for living in rural Mexico without a theater. But for me the trip meant shopping with Corque for new baseball gear.

When we returned home every year, Carlos, upon seeing the dust of an approaching vehicle long before it reached the barbed-wire fence that surrounded the land where the houses were built, would run out to open the gate. He greeted us with a big toothy smile. As soon as the Buick slowed to go through the gate, he would ask, "*Don Jorge, me trajo un guante nuevo?*"

My father would always make the same comment, "*Ya verás, ya verás, ten paciencia, muchacho.*"

THE FOLLOWING YEAR, CORQUE, MY GRANDMOTHER NATALIA, and I climbed into the old Buick to leave for El Paso at the end of May instead of late August. The trips had always been in August right before school started. My mother took pride in sending me to class in new clothes every year. But this year, she had been in El Paso for the past two months. I was about to get a baby brother or baby sister, and again, like so many Mexican families living close to the border, the expectant mother would stay with relatives in El Paso until the newborn arrived.

As her due date approached, Corque became more pensive, maybe even apprehensive. Without the usual commotion of the whole family or bundles of tamales and baskets of fruit in the car, I sat quietly in the front seat. Still pitch dark an hour later, just past the town of Galeana, the headlights fell on a thick, dark, moving blanket crossing the narrow highway. The tires were crunching the blanket and it sounded like popcorn popping.

"It's a mass of migrating tarantulas," Corque said in his cowboy drawl. He stopped the car and pulled out the battery-run lantern so Tita and I could see the sheet of creepy, hairy tarantulas as they ambled over the asphalt, apparently unperturbed by the car except, of course, for the ones trampled by the path of the tires.

"Tarantulas are large, eight-legged spiders named after a little southern Italian town called Taranto," my father explained. I looked down at them through the open window from the safety of the three-ton Buick.

"The terrestrial species, as we have here in the desert, make burrows in the ground and then they line the burrow wall with silk. The silk is really the spider web, just like any other spider web. It stabilizes the burrow wall and also helps the tarantula climb up and down the burrow," he continued to explain as I began to worry if they could spin enough webs to invade the car.

Corque opened the door to scoop up one of the hairy arachnids. He handed it to me. Instinctively I pulled away but Corque insisted, "Come on, Nati, it's not going to harm you. Even though they can bite, they usually don't unless they get really angry. They're not very poisonous even if they do bite. You know the men at the ranch handle them all the time. Don't tell me you're afraid."

"They scare me," I protested in a squeaky voice.

"It's not going to hurt you. Here, take it for a second so you can see it's just a harmless spider." Despite my squirming tightly into the door and against my grandmother's vocal objections from the rear seat, he took my hand and placed the tarantula in my palm.

"It tickles, Corque," I said. The tarantula crawled up my arm as I stopped breathing, afraid it would dig its great big jaws into the back of my neck and paralyze me forever if it detected the movement from my breath.

"Okay, now grab it with your other hand and throw it out the window," Corque instructed.

Taking it by a leg, I tried throwing it out the window, but instead of falling, it wrapped its free legs around my fingers. I screamed and hit my hand against the car door, smashing the tarantula into a slimy, hairy blob. I cried out in a desperate attempt to rid my hand of the sticky muck as Tita handed me a tissue to wipe the gooey mess off my hands, all the while reprimanding my father for his insensitive behavior.

Perceiving my fear, my father drove on, crunching more tarantulas for another hundred feet. On the ranch I played with frogs, tadpoles, toads, garden snakes, and turtles, picking them up and even taking them into the house to show my grandmother, the only one who appreciated my love of amphibians and reptiles. I also knew how to hook a wiggly worm on a fishing line, but the eerie sensation of thousands of tarantulas crawling under the Buick made my stomach queasy. The experience of holding one in my hand, staring down at it as it crawled up my arm, and killing it with my bare hand made me feel sick.

My father tried to smooth over the incident by reminding me how at the ranch, the cowboys would pit a brown tarantula against a black one. They would bet money on one or the other, just as they would bet on horses at the races. Except this was not a horse race, but an aggressive fight between two giant spiders. The tarantula fights could get just as rowdy as horse races with twenty to thirty men making bets, dropping money into baskets on the ground, yelling encouragement to the more aggressive tarantula or yelling obscenities, even louder, at the losing one.

As we drove over the endless desert road, I kept thinking how the hairy tarantulas reminded me of the thick, black hair peeking out from the half-open shirts the cowboys wore. I even wondered if all that hair might actually be tarantulas they had stuffed into their clothes to pull one out for a spontaneous spider fight.

I finally got my mind away from tarantulas when we arrived at *tía abuela*'s house in El Paso. I was happy to see my mother, even though she looked like the giant balloon in her belly might lift her into the air at any moment and fly off over the moon with her. After the initial happiness of seeing my mother, I discovered that this year, life was not the same. My mother complained about feeling uncomfortable and Corque was busy taking her to the doctor. They were gone for endless hours without so much as an explanation what they were doing. I felt completely left out.

Then the big event came and Corque bought cigars and bottles of whisky to give to his friends to celebrate the birth of the long-awaited son. "I finally have someone to inherit the ranch," he said proudly.

My father had time to tend to my mother, purchase all those boxes of liquor and cigars and boast with the people who came over to see the newborn, but we still had not purchased baseball equipment. Until this year, I had always thought the real purpose of the trip was to visit several stores, looking and comparing prices, quality and brands to select our baseball gear. Now Corque had a tiny, screaming, colicky baby who seemed to take all his attention. Baseball was obviously not the reason for this year's trip. And not to mention my mother. Every bit of her time revolved around that baby. I had to be quiet as he slept; I had to be still if he was crying and I could not jump around the bassinet at any time. I even had to fetch clean diapers so my mother could change him.

My grandmother was the only one who cared for me anymore. She alone, seeing the hurt in my eyes, took me for a walk.

"Corque has forgotten that we always get new balls and bats when we come to El Paso. He only seems interested in that baby," I complained.

"He's been busy with the baby and with your Mom, but he'll take you shopping before we return home," she assured me.

"Tita, I think my father has forgotten about me and baseball. He's only thinking about playing baseball with the baby."

My grandmother laughed. "Do you really think he's going to play baseball with the baby?"

"Yes, he is," I replied, tears welling up in my eyes. "I would like to take those tarantulas we saw on the highway and put them in the baby's crib so they can gobble him up! That way, I can...," but my grandmother interrupted me, not letting me finish my thought.

"Nati, what a mean thing to say. You must not be serious about that, Sweetie."

"Oh, yes I am serious. I want that baby out of my life," I yelled.

"What is it that bothers you about your little brother?" Tita asked. She stroked my hair trying to calm me.

"Everything," I said, tears flowing down my cheeks. "He has taken Corque away from me. You see that he's even taken my mother away from me. Corque will take my horse and he'll give it to that ugly, screaming, red-faced baby."

"Your father would never take Vago back from you."

"Yes, he will. He gave that ugly baby his own name. His own name! The baby is Jorge, just like my Corque," I said, crying.

"We all love you, Nati. Your little brother is not going to take anyone away from you," my grandmother said. She tried to comfort me, putting her arms around me and hugging me tightly. "He just needs more help right now because he was just born."

"If Corque still loves me, then why doesn't he take me to buy bats and balls for me and Carlos to play baseball? Corque is not going to play ball with me anymore. I know it. I know he's only going to play baseball with the baby," I sobbed, my whole body shaking in anger.

"Well, let's see," she said. She consoled me as she wiped my tears away. "I don't think your little brother can hold a bat or even stand up at home plate. He can't even see very well yet, so he couldn't see the ball being pitched. It'll take about five years before he'll be able to play baseball and by then, you'll be fourteen. You will be in high school and you'll probably be more interested in boys than baseball."

"Interested in boys? Why, Tita, what a silly thing to say."

"In any case," she said, "if you're still playing baseball, you will want to do so with your friends and not with your father."

We walked for several blocks allowing time for me to calm down. Tita spoke about the apple blossoms and the Spanish Broom blooming in people's yards and how it reminded her of her own childhood. She reminisced out loud about her brothers and the memories of games they played and how they took care of her every time she fell off a horse. "You will find that brothers are really okay once you get used to them and they get a little older."

As we turned the corner to *tía abuela*'s house, Corque came out to meet us. "Are you ready to check out baseball gear?" he asked me.

I looked up at Tita, smiled and ran towards the Buick. As I opened the door, a big, black tarantula jumped out, landing near my feet. The hairy desert hitchhiker must have found its way across the border in the old Buick with us. I stomped on it, scraped the sole of my shoe on the concrete driveway and turned back to look at Corque. "Yes, I'm ready," I said, climbing in the front seat.

Juan Bobo

by Nelson Denis

DELFONSO SOLÁ MORALES STADIUM HAD SIX thousand seats, two hundred paying customers, and fifty skinny boys sitting on the right field wall. They shimmied up a palm tree and waved dozens of broomsticks with butterfly nets on the end. They rarely got a ball, though. The *Criollos de Caguas* had not hit a home run in two years. When the owner sold the team to run for mayor, both he and his opponent had the same platform: to scrap the team and demolish the stadium. After the election they changed their mind.

The field was full of holes, ruts, and countless other hazards. An ant colony wiggled under first base. Insects bigger than silver dollars bounced off the bulbs and zoomed around all the players. Two panels behind home plate were covered with cardboard. Out in right field, just below the butterfly nets, a sloping mound of red dirt served as the outfield fence and behind it (to keep out the boys) a twelve-foot wall of barbed wire topped a pile of garbage cans filled with broken beer bottles and a narrow hole, partially covered with Johnson grass, that was home to a rattlesnake.

The fans didn't care. Half of them were busy selling something to the other half: old women sold barbecue chicken and *alcapúrrias* in the bleachers, old men sold *cocos fríos* near the bullpen, and kids sold cigarettes, chewing tobacco, Chiclets, and stolen baseball caps to everyone. An eight-year old sold *Coronas* from a hidden bucket. Down on the infield, a boy in a torn Mickey Mouse T-shirt shuffled through the dugouts selling *negritos,* thimble-sized cups of strong sweetened coffee, to the players themselves.

A scratchy rendition of *La Borinqueña* brought the selling to a pause. Even the boys on the fence stood up, their poles held aloft like lances, for the Puerto Rican national anthem.

"Play *bol!*" yelled an ump, but no one paid attention as firecrackers exploded under the bleachers and a *bomba y plena* band snaked its way through the stands.

"Play bol *coño!*" he yelled again, and the first batter from the *Indios de Mayaguez* stepped up to the plate. The game went as usual. Don Q hit two *Indios* in the head. Pitrós crashed through a wall. Wilson stole the *Indios* running signals and then a catcher's mitt. A huge fight broke out, the *Criollos de Caguas* forfeited the game, seven of them went to jail, and all of them demanded to speak with Juan Bobo.

HE WAS IN A DEEP TRANCE WITH A HOCKEY HELMET ON HIS HEAD and a potted salvia divinorum plant in his lap. The helmet was stuffed with magnets, electrodes and wiring all plugged into a telephone, which was plugged into a shortwave radio, which was plugged into a TV.

"Zzzzzzzzzzz..."

Juan was asleep. A test pattern showed on the TV. Several life-like dummies hung from the hot water pipes. One of them was bleeding, another wore a crown of thorns, a third one was headless and wore a bridal gown. A case of *Pétrus* and *Romanée-Conti* flanked either side of the door. Otherwise the room was piled high with books about...sleep.

The *Oneirocritica,* the *Upanishads,* William Blake, Freud, Jung, Emanuel Swedenborg, Robert L. Van de Castle, eighteen dream theorists, and countless sleep studies filled the entire basement. For days he'd sit there with his salvia plant, tinkering with the hockey helmet, rolling his eyes into his head and falling into a deep REM sleep.

Deep down inside, his mother believed he was masturbating. His sister knew he was smoking salvia. The *Criollos* were convinced he was hiding their money. The rest of the town whispered about witchcraft. But Juan was not a *Babalawo,* not yet. That would come later.

"Oye, Juan, you deaf or something?"

"Wha-?"

"Wake up, you bum. And quit smoking that stuff. You're killing mami."

"I'll kill you first."

"I swear to God, I'm going to throw that thing away."

Juan grabbed the plant and glared at his sister. She stood there like a drill sergeant, hands on her hips, on top of the basement stairs.

"You leave Agnes alone," Juan said. "How did you get in here?"

"Wilson's calling."

"Tell him to call back."

"I don't think so."

"What?"

"He's in jail with half of the team."

"Good for him."

"You're kidding, right?"

"No, I'm sleeping. Goodbye."

His sister stared at him, then noticed a book on top of the *Romanée-Conti*. "Did you steal this book?"

"Vete ya, sangre gorda! And thanks for knocking."

"You're welcome. You look like Frankenstein in that helmet."

She stomped out and slammed the door. Juan took off his hockey helmet, perched Agnes on the TV, and picked up a few tools. Within two hours he'd installed the most medieval security system known to man. Not even the Devil would penetrate that door.

HIS NAME WAS SERGEANT PAPO ESTRADA, BUT ALL THE prisoners called him Papo Bullshit. As a lifelong alcoholic he was often in jail and had been a model prisoner. He knew how a jail should be run. In fact, Papo knew more about jail than anyone.

No one understood how he managed to become a cop. But when a man was in jail, Papo would bring him a little wine, sit in the cell with him, and start to tell him stories. Papo knew more stories than a hundred other men. Sometimes if they drank enough wine, Papo would forget he was the jailer...and he and the prisoner would both escape. Needless to say, Papo Bullshit was the most popular policeman in the history of Caguas.

When seven *Criollos de Caguas* were arrested on February 9th, Papo hauled out eight gallons of Manischewitz, never mind from where.

"*Hola, amigos*, welcome back! Did you hear what happened to Chicharra and his home care attendant?"

The ballplayers took heart, listening to Papo's stories and anticipating an early release. But the evening took a serious turn as the first gallon brought on sober conversation. The second gallon, sweetly sad memory. The third gallon, thoughts of lost loves. The fourth gallon, thoughts of Nancy Greenblatt, the faithless bitch with coconut tits. The fifth gallon, serious doubts about God. The sixth gallon, plans of blackest revenge. The seventh gallon, songs of death and suicide. The *Criollos de Caguas* didn't want to open the eighth gallon. They certainly didn't want to finish it. They just wanted Juan Bobo to get them the hell out of there.

"MY NAME IS PAPO BULLSHIT, AND YOU'RE ALL UNDER ARREST."

"We're already in jail."

"My name is Papo Bullshit, *y me cago en tu madre.*"

"Not here you won't."

"My name is Papo Bullshit..."

And so it went for sixteen hours. They'd finished the Manischewitz, all eight gallons of it, and still no one had escaped. Papo the jailer (aka Papo Bullshit) had gotten plastered, tried to hang himself and when they yanked him down, his keys flew out of the cell...sixteen hours, eight men, one broken toilet. By the time Juan walked in, the *Criollos de Caguas* were ready to kill somebody.

"*Coño!*"

"*Te voy a romper la cara!*"

"You call yourself a manager?"

Juan Bobo spat on the floor. "This is the third time this month. You're lucky I came at all."

"If you bought us some equipment, we wouldn't have to steal it!"

"*Pendejo!*"

"You call yourself a manager?"

"You call yourself a ballplayer? Where the hell is Papo?"

Papo was snoring like an elephant behind the toilet, and within two minutes the *Criollos de Caguas* were free. As a man of honor Juan left $20 on Papo's chest for the eight gallons of Manischewitz. Then he gave $100 to Choco Ruiz, along with the usual instructions.

CHOCO SAT IN A FOLDING CHAIR AND WAVED TO HIS FANS. THEY were losing by 12-1 to the worst team in the league, but Choco had no shame. He cooled himself with a little motorized fan and blew kisses to women in the stands.

"Whatever you need, just come to Choco!"

What they needed was some talent. Roberto Clemente had been a *Criollo*. The team had won fourteen Puerto Rico pennants and three Caribbean World Series, but you'd never know it by this bunch.

Don Q, the starting pitcher, had a 98 mph fastball but was usually half-drunk and utterly unpredictable.

Pitrós, the catcher, had a huge family to feed and was the hardest working *Criollo*. He had two concussions and four cracked ribs from chasing foul balls into the stands. When money got tight he would bet on the other team, but everyone forgave him because he hustled so much.

Flaco Navaja, the first baseman, was very mean-tempered and known to stab base runners.

Bambino was a lazy second baseman, but the best hitter on the team.

Perico had a cocaine habit and autonomic dysreflexia, which sent him into seizures at shortstop. This was helpful in hit and run situations but otherwise useless.

Wilson the third baseman had no arm, was the worst fielder on the team, but had an uncanny ability to steal running signals and the other team's equipment.

Papa Cool was black as coal and showed some actual talent in center field. He could run like the wind and usually had to, because the other outfielders refused to chase any fly balls. If the spirit moved him, and the opposing team catcher had a hangover, Papa Cool could steal two bases on a single pitch.

Manolete the left fielder was the laziest player of all, so lazy that he wouldn't even swing the bat. God forbid he should connect...'cause then he'd have to run. He developed a superb eye at the plate, and had the second highest base-on-balls percentage in the entire league. Every time he got a close call from the ump, Manolete's fans would yell "*¡Olé!*"

El Sapo the right fielder was built like a frog: fat, four and one-half feet tall, with a head as big as his torso. Sapo couldn't hit to save his life but, when he crouched, his entire strike zone was smaller than a salad plate. He had the *highest* base-on-balls percentage in the entire league.

And then came Choco, the substitute infielder. He played once every twenty games and was perfectly happy. "Bench me or trade me!" he yelled, whenever he appeared in two consecutive starting lineups. After a rigorous spring training workout he told a reporter "I can't wait for the season to start, so I can get some rest."

The fans loved Choco. He turned uselessness into an art form, and so they identified with him. He showed up at every game with custom-made alligator-skin spikes, a folding chair, and a pillow for extra comfort. He sat outside the dugout and cooled himself with a handheld electric fan, signing baseballs all night long. But Choco had one more talent.

A Tarot card lady gave free readings to every player on the visiting team. Through a series of signals, she communicated to Choco which ones had a girlfriend in town, or were looking for one. By the end of the game Choco had sold a girl, watch, ring, or bracelet to every one of those players. The Tarot card lady got season tickets, Choco and Juan Bobo split the profits, and everyone was happy.

"Run, you lazy bastard!"

Manolete had ducked a high fast one, and hit the ball by accident. The pitcher fielded it, rolled the ball along the infield grass, and still beat Manolete by ten feet.

"What are you, a Mack truck?"

"Get that bum outta there!"

The fans had seen enough, and started throwing mangos out onto the field. Juan was shaking his head in the dugout when Cartucho the Midget plopped down next to him.

"You got my money yet?" said the midget.

"Not here."

"The hell with that. It's been two weeks!"

"How'd you get in here?"

"Never mind."

"You know something, Cartucho? If you weren't a midget I'd beat the crap out of you right here."

"Money, please."

"You got some nerve."

Cartucho picked up a baseball bat and the whole bench started laughing. The bat was bigger than he was.

"Dame mi' chávo', muerdealmohadas!"

"Are you crazy?"

"I wear a wedding dress for you. I fly out the window. I dig under the trees and bark like a dog. And I...want...my... MONEY!"

He smashed the water cooler and drenched half the team. "Get that shrimp out of here!" they yelled, so Juan pulled out a few dollars and stuffed them in Cartucho's hand.

"You happy now?"

"What do you call this?"

"A down payment."

"Are you freakin' kidding me?"

"I'm saving money for my mother's operation."

"She's been having the same operation for twenty years!"

"You better watch your mouth."

"Or what?" Cartucho sneered and spit in the dugout. "I'm not afraid of you. And I'm sick and tired of hearing about your mother."

"We'll talk later tonight."

"No more talk! I...want...my..."

"You'll get your money, I just don't have it here."

"Where is it?"

"At home."

"No me jodas, Juan!"

"You're my partner, I wouldn't do that."

"At home."

"That's right."

"Tonight."

"Whenever."

"No me jodas, Juan!"

The park went wild. Bambino hit a wicked line drive, all the way to the garbage cans in right field. He got on his horse and reached second for a stand-up double. Unfortunately Manolete was standing there too, and they were both tagged out. The whole stadium groaned and another wave of mangos went sailing onto the field. A few of them crashed into the dugout. Juan ducked a mango, turned, and Cartucho was gone.

AS OF FEBRUARY 14, 2008, THE PUERTO RICO WINTER LEAGUE standings were as follows:

Team	Won	Lost	Pct.	G.B.
Barones de Barceloneta	36	12	.750	--
Cangregeros de Santurce	32	16	.667	4
Gigantes de Carolina	27	21	.562	9
Indios de Mayaguez	24	24	.500	12
Lobos de Arecibo	21	27	.438	15
Criollos de Caguas	16	32	.333	20
Leones de Ponce	12	36	.250	24

With an incredible .750 win percentage, the *Barones de Barceloneta* were the best team in Puerto Rico, maybe in the 70-year history of the entire league. They were sponsored by Pfizer Pharmaceutical, since all of the Viagra consumed in North America (the U.S., Canada and Mexico) was produced in one huge factory in Barceloneta. The plant manager, Adam Clayton Powell VII, was also the manager of the baseball team.

The *Criollos* were another story. The fans were shocked whenever they won a game, and hurled vegetables at Juan every time they lost. Juan wanted to quit, but he hung on because *mami* needed the money, and because baseball is a great game for redemption, since it's so full of failure. Just like life.

On February 14, the *Barones* marched into Ydelfonso Solá Morales Stadium in grand fashion. *¡Viva Viagra!* played on the P.A. Powell waved like a politician. An African Bush

Elephant paraded around the entire field and left a large present in front of the *Criollos de Caguas* dugout.

"*¡Ai fo'!*"

"*¡Ea rayo!*"

"*¿Quien trajo ese pinche elefante?*"

Old Man Oye, a tiny old man, walked slowly and leaned hard on a cane. People patted him on the back and his narrow shoulders sagged, as he limped to his spot behind the *Criollos* dugout. Juan Bobo's old friends—the butcher, the banker, and the priest from the Holy Agony—sat right behind him, and threw peanuts at the elephant.

Way out in right field lay Filadelfo the accordion player, wrapped in a tattered blanket, sleeping off a drunk. Filadelfo had toured with Mantovani, but now he played only one tune when intoxicated—"*En Mi Viejo San Juan.*" When very drunk he also remembered fragments of Mendelssohn's *Spring Song.* As the only high-brow musician in all of Caguas, Filadelfo possessed a just celebrity. He was brilliant and industrious—his sons and daughters were innumerable—but the artistic temperament was too much for him.

They woke up Filadelfo, then everyone stood for "*La Borinqueña,*" and the mayor of Caguas marched up in a frock coat and silk top hat, to name Adam Clayton Powell VII the "Citizen of the Year." It was probably for the elephant, which had doubled the day's attendance to nearly five hundred.

"Play *bol*!"

The first batter stepped up. As Don Q started his wind-up a dwarf honked a loud horn, Don Q hesitated, an ump yelled "bok!"...and just like that, the *Barones* were on first base. Before a pitch was ever thrown.

"*¡Vaya Don Q!*"

"Have another drink!"

"I want my money back!"

Don Q swayed a moment. He was indeed half-drunk, and the fumes from the elephant dung weren't helping any, so he made his own contribution by throwing up on the mound. "Livin' *la Vida Loca*" played on the stadium P.A. as they cleaned up the mess. The mayor stopped smiling and stared at Juan.

The next batter drove Don Q crazy. He left the batter's box on each and every pitch, tugged endlessly on his gloves, tapped his helmet, kicked his feet, grabbed his crotch, spit, pointed the bat at Don Q's head, made the sign of the cross, kissed his hand, pointed to heaven, then stepped back into the batter's box and repeated the ritual all over *again*. Don Q was miserable, smelling the elephant and the vomit, and he started to sweat.

"Ball one."

"*¡Vamos, coño!*" yelled Pitrós at the batter, as he strolled away and repeated his whole routine. It worked like a charm. Three pitches later he flipped his bat and trotted to first.

The dwarf honked his horn again.

"*Oye, cabrón,* I got a family to feed," yelled Pitrós at his pitcher. "You better throw some strikes, or *ite rompo el culo!*" Don Q got the hint. Three fastballs hit Pitrós like a cannon, froze their clean-up man, and the fans showed their appreciation.

"¡Vaya Don Q!"

"Have another drink!"

The next batter blasted a line drive right into Wilson's glove, the finest play he'd made all season.

The dwarf honked his horn again, but Don Q ignored him. Nothing much happened over the next three innings so Choco Ruiz set up a folding chair, turned on his little fan, and started blowing kisses into the crowd. A pitcher's duel developed and Don Q followed the only strategy he knew...fastball, fastball, fastball.

To everyone's surprise, the teams were tied 2-2 after sixteen innings, and the mayor of Caguas went home.

The dwarf honked his horn again in the top of the eighteenth with the bases loaded, as a batter the size of a sofa lumbered up to the plate. Don Q stopped the game, marched into the dugout, and demanded a bottle of rum. Old Man Oye leaned over the rail and passed him some Bacardi.

"Gracias, viejo," said Don Q, and walked over to Juan Bobo.

"Hey coach, what's that?"

"Huh?"

"That."

He pointed the Bacardi toward the *Barones*.

"I think that's the other team."

"No, look higher."

Juan looked and saw a dwarf in toddler overalls, and a T-shirt that said "Scotty Berg ♥ Ayn Rand." The dwarf clutched an old horn, taped to a two-foot walking stick.

"You see the dwarf?"

"Who, Scotty Berg?"

"Yeah. He's been blasting that thing all day."

"I know."

"At me."

"Yup."

"It's getting on my nerves."

"So have a drink."

"That's it?"

"Yeah."

He took three gulps and winked at Juan. "One for each pitch," he said. Then he jogged back to the mound, threw his gyro-ball, and twisted the sofa-sized batter into a pretzel.

When the *Criollos* fanned to end the eighteenth, the umpire waved the managers over to home plate. Adam Clayton Powell VII refused to accept a tie, and stared at Juan the whole time. "This isn't over," he said.

JUAN BOBO GULPED SOME BACARDI THAT NIGHT, AND WALKED down an empty street. "This isn't over," he muttered, over and over again.

Juan lived on the poor side of the *Expreso de Las Américas* Highway. On the other side was the *Caguas Real* Golf and Country Club, stuffed with doctors and pharmaceutical reps, surrounded by streets with ridiculous names like *Calle Buckingham, Calle Windsor, Calle Tudor, Calle Edinburgo* and *Calle Luxemburgo*...as if to confer some British nobility on their residents, and a Manifest Destiny on their greed.

But tonight he renamed his own streets, the ones that he lived in. Tonight he carried a tool box, a small ladder and some metal signs that read *Calle Hope*. The signs were professionally engraved and didn't cost much, just a few baseball tickets for Bobby Capó's Pawn Shop. Over the past two years he'd nailed up *Calle Faith*, *Calle Humility*, *Calle Equality*, and he had a few more *Calles* to go. The last one would be *Calle Love*.

It was a one-man campaign, renaming the streets in his neighborhood in the middle of the night. Aside from helping his mother it was the one thing he was proud of. He didn't ask anyone for permission because he knew he wouldn't get it. But he knew he had to do it. A man should never allow others to choose his words, or name the streets he lived in. That night, Juan turned three dark streets into *Calle Hope*.

When he got home he found his sister Barbie, twirling before the bathroom mirror. She was modeling her finest dresses, tweezing her eyebrows, puckering her lips, singing show tunes from *West Side Story*.

"What's going on?"

"Nothing."

"Why all this singing?"

"I'm going to a party."

"Hmm...don't do anything stupid."

Barbie closed the door and sang even louder.

THE NEXT DAY THE AFRICAN BUSH ELEPHANT MARCHED INTO THE baseball stadium again, wearing a huge blue sign:

Barónes de Barceloneta Bash

Everyone welcome, drinks courtesy of Viagra
10 pm tonight
Caguas Real Country and Golf Club
700 Alhambra Blvd.

At every entrance, a Pfizer employee passed out fliers for the event. In all the grandstands, a regiment of "Diamond Girls" handed out complimentary packets of Viagra. A *Barones* mascot ran around the infield.

"What the hell is going on?" said Juan.

"Don't ask me," said Choco Ruiz. "But that mascot looks like a giant penis with a wig."

Choco liked being the center of attention, and yelled a few choice words at the mascot. But Juan sensed something deeper: Adam Clayton Powell VII was trying to steal the stadium, and maybe Juan's job.

"Play *bol*!"

Don Q was drunker than the day before, and hit the first batter with a 98 mph fast ball. The benches emptied out and the elephant rose on his hind legs, as a fight broke out all over the field. Choco Ruiz turned on his little battery-powered fan and watched it all from his folding chair.

"Play *bol*!"

Don Q was sweating like a pig, but he bore down and retired the *Barones* one, two, three. Then the *Criollos* got mowed down. Three innings later the score was still 2-2, and the dwarf started honking his horn.

"Ah shit, I want some rum," said Don Q.

"Like hell," said Juan and motioned to Bambino, who was squatting in the on-deck circle.

"Yeah coach?"

"What do you think of that dwarf?"

"He's a pain the ass."

"You ever seen him before?"

"No."

"Me neither. I think he's working for them."

"It wouldn't surprise me."

"How are you feeling today?"

"*Chévere.*"

"Good. Hit the dwarf."

"What?

"Hit the dwarf."

"Okay."

Bambino walked out calmly, and slammed the first pitch past the dwarf's nose.

"Aiieeeeeeeee!" shrieked the dwarf.

The next ball headed straight for the dwarf's teeth, but he ducked and it hit a rail behind him.

"Aiieeeeeeeee!"

Bambino chopped a third foul...it took off like a shot and hit the dwarf's skull with a dull thud. The little man dropped his horn, and was never heard from again.

The pitchers dueled for several more innings and Choco was having the time of his life. He sat with his little fan, selling jewelry to the *Barones* through the Tarot card lady, and blowing kisses at the "Diamond Girls." For several scoreless innings he tutored two of them on the merits of combining Viagra with marijuana, Grey Goose, and clove cigarettes.

Disaster struck in the twenty eighth inning. When the *Barones* pitcher laid down a bunt, the first and third basemen *should* have charged the plate, the pitcher *should* have covered first, the second baseman and shortstop *should* have covered second and third, the outfielders *should* have charged in to back up every base. Instead the *Criollos* all stood around until the runner was rounding first, then Wilson overthrew the ball into right field, then El Sapo slipped on an elephant turd, then Papa Cool missed the cutoff man, and the pitcher turned a bunt into an inside-the-park home run.

"Go home, you bums!"

"*¿Qué pasa, maricón?*"

"I want my money back!"

A hail of mangos and blackened bananas hit the field. The game stopped for twenty minutes as the ground crew cleared the infield, the elephant ate the bananas, and the *Barones* laughed uncontrollably. When they finally got their licks, two *Criollos* grounded out and Papa Cool took two quick strikes. The bat looked like a sagging baloney in Papa's hands. The *Barones* all chuckled. And then a miracle happened.

Papa somehow lofted a high fly to center field. It was a routine play, but the sun was setting and it blinded the outfielder. By the time they recovered the ball and fired it, Papa had crossed the plate. *"¡Que viva el negrito!"* howled the whole stadium.

A few innings later, the ump called the managers over.

"Listen, gentlemen. It's 3-3 after thirty four innings. I've never seen anything like it. Let's call it a tie."

"No!" said Powell.

"But—"

"This game isn't over."

"It is if we say so—"

"And I say no!"

Powell stared at Juan the whole time. Maybe he shouldn't have sold Powell the hat. The ump turned to Juan.

"What do you think, Mr. Bobo?"

"I think it's ridiculous. We've got twelve more games on our schedule. What do we do, just shut down the whole league?"

"My company owns this damn league."

"Well you don't own *me*. So why don't you take your Viagra, give it to your damn elephant, and get the hell out of here?"

A raggedy ball boy came huffing to the plate. "Mr. Bobo, you have a call."

"Later."

"I think you better take this."

"Hmm. Excuse me, gentlemen." Juan smiled into Powell's red face and walked to the dugout.

"Hello."

"Juan Bobo?"

"That's me."

"This is Willie Miranda Marín, the mayor of Caguas."

"Oh, hi."

"I'm sitting here with Remy."

"Remy who?"

"Remy Garcia, your League Commissioner."

"Hello, Remy."

"We're very proud of you, Juan."

"Why's that?"

"Have you ever heard of the Rochester Red Wings?"

"No."

"Cal Ripken played with them in 1981."

"Oh."

"But wait, there's more. In 1981, the Rochester Red Wings played against the Pawtucket Red Sox. The game lasted three days...the longest game in professional baseball history."

"Wow."

"So guess what?"

"What."

"Are you sitting down?"

"No."

"Well maybe you better. That game lasted thirty-three innings. You've just gone thirty-four."

"You mean—"

"That's right, my friend. You are now playing the longest game in the history of professional baseball!"

"Ay Dios mío."

"Isn't that great?"

"I was hoping to end this game."

"What? Are you crazy? We're going to make a fortune!"

"My players are exhausted."

"Your players are getting paid, and they're making history."

"So what happens now?"

"You just keep playing, we'll take care of the rest."

The phone went dead a moment, then Commissioner Remy Garcia came on the line.

"Juan, you still there?"

"Yeah."

"Listen, we don't care who wins the game. Just give us some good clean baseball."

"What do you mean?"

"No fighting, no drinking."

"Oh, please."

"Well...do the best you can."

"Yes, sir. And how about the elephant?"

"What about it?"

"It's hurting our game."

"It's also doubling our stadium receipts. Next year *you're* getting an elephant."

"I can't be responsible for what happens."

"No one said you were. The elephant stays."

"Bueno."

"One more thing: I want all the players at the Viagra party tonight."

"Wait a minute-"

"Ten o'clock at the Caguas Country Club."

"We're trying to win a ballgame!"

"And we're trying to make some money, for a change."

"But—"

"Ten o'clock."

Tomboy Forgiveness

by David Rice

**ET READY, 'CAUSE THIS IS GONNA KNOCK YOU** over," Tía Berta said with a sly grin as she leaned over the pitching mound with the eager softball in her hand.

Our mother, standing firm over home plate, swirled her bat and spit. "You can't strike me out," she said. When my sister, Rosana, and I saw Mom spit, we knew she was going to hit the ball with all her strength so we backed up. Berta adjusted her baseball cap, kicked some dirt off the pitching mound, and spun her arm in a blur and the ball shot out like a cannonball. In one quick move Mom pulled and swung the bat at full speed and slammed the ball in our direction.

"I got it," Rosana shouted, and the ball smacked her glove. She raised the ball in the air, "It's still hot."

Mom adjusted her cap. "Think I'm ready for the tournament this weekend?" she said with a wide smile.

Berta let out a booming laugh and kicked dirt off the pitching mound like a bull ready to charge. "Girl, you and me. In the final," she said.

Berta was our Mom's best friend even though they played softball against each other with every fiber in their being. We called Berta Tía Berta because we saw her so much, and she was also our mother's hairdresser and made sure our Mom was the only Mexican-American woman in town with bright blond hair or cherry red hair. Every three months Mom walked into the house with a new color and a new attitude. "Keep them guessing," she'd say, and she was the same way in softball.

You never knew what she was going to do. Line drive, bunt, grounder, or hit a home run. But you weren't going to be ready. Our father said the same about her. "*Esta mujer,*" he'd say in frustration, but every year his brake shop sponsored Mom's softball team with new uniforms and equipment. The only catch was, he liked to be third-base coach, and he was good at yelling and swinging his arms like a deranged monkey. At every game he'd shout orders like a bully. The softball team lasted longer than their marriage.

When we were little, Mom and Dad were always fighting and then all of a sudden he found a new wife and a new family. We knew the brand-new sons because they were our age and we saw them at school all the time. It was something we got used to, and by the time we got to junior high everybody knew the story, so it didn't bother us too much. When our parents divorced, it was Berta who was by our mother's side through the whole ordeal, and she did her best to cheer Mom up.

Our hometown of Edcouch hosted the softball tournament, and teams from Elsa, La Villa, Monte Alto, La

Blanca, Hargil, Santa Rosa, and Weslaco filled up our ballpark. Edcouch only had 2,656 people, but during the tournament our town doubled in size.

Every year Mom and Tía Berta were the rock stars of the tournament, and people shook their hands as they walked by. Mom was the best hitter in the league, and Tia Berta the best pitcher. When Beto's Brake Shop played against Berta's Beauty Shop, the bleachers would get packed with fans cheering for both teams. There were no losers.

One week before the tournament, the Rubén pony express broke down and Rosana got some messed-up news. Rosana was in eighth grade, and she had a class with Rubén, our dad's stepson. They got along OK, and Mom used Rubén as a post office. If Mom wanted to send a message to Dad she'd write it down on a piece of paper, seal it in an envelope and give it to Rosana. Rosana would give it to Rubén, and Rubén gave it to Dad. It wasn't very mature, but the postage was free.

I was walking down the school halls between classes when Rosana came barreling toward me, brushing kids aside like a hurricane with the latest news. She took my arm and pushed me against the wall.

"Guess what Rubén just told me?" she said like it was the most important thing she ever heard.

I jerked my arm from her grasp. "What, that he wets the bed?"

"Pffff. Grosero." Then in a secret hush, she said, "He told me that Dad is seeing some other woman."

"What?" I said.

"Yeah, Rubén said that his mom kicked Dad out the house," Rosana said.

"Ah, man, are you serious?" I said with a chuckle, 'cause I thought it was kinda funny.

"Yeah, and you'll never guess who Dad is seeing."

I shrugged my shoulders. "Who?"

Rosana took a deep breath and shook her head in disbelief. "Tía Berta."

You know how in cartoons when someone gets hit on the head with a frying pan and their head vibrates, making ringing sounds? That's what I felt like when my sister told me that Dad was seeing Tía Berta.

"What?" I grabbed my sister's arms to keep my head from shaking to pieces.

"I know, I know. It's so messed up," she said.

"Does Mom know?" I said.

"I don't know."

"What are we going to do?" I said.

My sister let out a sigh. "Poor Mom," she said.

The rest of the day I walked in a daze, turning over the possibilities of Mom's reaction. Even though my parents were divorced and all, it was still uncool what Tía Berta was doing, but at the same time it wasn't any of my business. That afternoon my sister and I walked home together, something we didn't do often, but we needed each other. It was Monday night softball practice and we thought that probably one of Mom's teammates would tell her the news. When we got home we decided to clean up the house real nice so if Mom came home in a bad mood, at least the house was clean. By 5:30 Mom wasn't home yet and we called her cell phone, but she didn't answer.

"Do you think Mom knows?" I asked my sister.

Rosana threw her arms up. "By now the whole town knows," she said

It was close to 10:00 when Mom walked in the house. We were watching TV and we stood up. She was wearing her softball practice clothes and she was covered in sweat. I don't remember my parent's divorce, but what I was feeling must have been what I felt when our father left us. Mom wears her emotions like a jacket. Everyone can see what she's thinking.

"Mom, you okay?" my sister asked.

"You guys heard, huh?"

We nodded.

"I ran four miles after practice. You know how it is. You just gotta sweat it out." She pulled her head back and exhaled. Then she brought her head down and shook it like boxers do before a fight. "I'm just going to stay focused on the tournament."

The next day a few of her teammates came to the house to go over the batting order. Mom's softball friends were loud and loved to drink beer out of bottles as they decided who would hit singles, doubles, and home runs. Tía Berta was usually there to help out with the list since she knew the batting styles of every player, but not this time. Her name wasn't even mentioned and her laugh didn't fill our house. All week long there was this dark cloud hanging over Mom. I had never seen her look so sad, and I knew that the tournament was going to be make-or-break for her.

Saturday morning was gloomy, and there were low dark clouds as far as you could see. Mom had her game face on, and so did my sister. Rosana was the bat girl and equipment manager, and took her jobs seriously. My job was to mix Gatorade in a big cooler with lots of ice, and stay out of their way as we loaded Mom's truck. I rode in the back of the truck surrounded by mesh nylon bags of gear for the short drive to the City of Edcouch Ball Park. Four fields of hard-hitting softball action. The tournament was fast. Only eight teams with four fields and double elimination, and each game with a time limit of one hour and fifteen minutes.

When we parked, Mom's teammates walked up with the game schedule. The first team they would play was Berta's Beauty Shop. Mom nodded. "Well then, they will be the first team to lose." When both teams stood in line on the field for the "Star-Spangled Banner," you could feel the frustration between the teams. It was strange because the players were all friends and many of them had grown up together, but they didn't know how to act. Fans were at a loss too, but secretly they were taking sides. But in the end, everyone knew the game would have the answers.

Our father stayed away from Mom, and Berta stayed away from our father. My sister and I said very little, and cheering for Beto's Brake Shop didn't feel right because we felt like we were cheering for our father, since his name was on their uniforms. The game started off with Berta pitching the first strikeout of the day. You could see Berta taking the game seriously and doing her best, but she couldn't strike Mom out.

Each time Mom was up to bat she got on base. With four minutes left in the game, Berta's Beauty Shop was up by one. Our father made short paces behind third base, clapping his hands. "Come on, the clock is ticking."

Mom's team had one runner on second and our mother was up to bat. Mom picked up some dirt and rubbed her hands. Berta adjusted her cap and put the ball right down the middle. "Strike one," the umpire shouted. Mom took a step back and moved her head side to side and then returned to the batter's box with the bat pulled back tight. Berta pitched a blur, and the umpire shouted, "Strike two." Mom took a step back and gave her bat a couple of short swings and then got ready for Berta's third pitch. Berta threw low, but this time Mom's bat was there to say hello and goodbye.

The ball sailed deep into right field, and the woman on second scrambled home. Mom sprinted through first and rounded second before the outfielder threw the ball in. Our father was shouting, "Go, go, go! Take it home!" My sister and I were standing, shouting the same thing along with the crowd. Mom blew through third, and Berta caught the ball and threw it hard to home. As the ball touched the catcher's glove, Mom slammed her and the ball shot out of the glove.

"Safe!" the umpire shouted, with one minute left on the clock as Mom and the catcher hit the ground. There was a roar of cheers from the stands. Berta's Beauty Shop advanced to the loser's bracket, and Beto's Brake Shop advanced to the winner's bracket.

By noon, my sister and I had sore throats from all the yelling and shouting. Mom's team couldn't make a mistake if they tried. Meanwhile, Berta's team was on a winning streak in the loser's bracket. Talk throughout the tournament was about a final game between Beto's Brake Shop and Berta's Beauty Shop, and each game moved Mom and Berta closer. Mom's team cut Juanita's Flower shop to pieces, and Berta's team burned down The Hot Tamale House. Usually the teams who lost would leave, but everyone knew that the final game was more than just a game, and lots of people got on their cell phones, and even more people showed up.

My sister told me that people were betting to see who would win the tournament, and some were even betting that our Mom and Tía Berta would get into a fistfight.

"What?" I said.

"You know that Mom and Tía Berta were big tomboys," My sister said with a worried look. "We need to talk to Mom."

Five minutes before the final game, we told Mom about the bets going around.

Mom smacked her fist into her glove. "I'll bet your father started those stupid bets."

"But Mom, you're not going to get into a fight with Tía Berta, are you?" my sister asked.

Mom looked shocked. "Berta is my best friend. I would never hurt her."

"But you're not talking to her. And all your friends are mad at her," I said.

"But I'm not mad at her," Mom said. "I'm just hurt." She could see we were worried. "Hey, it's going to be OK. I'm not going to let your father ruin this, too. Just cheer for Berta like you cheer for me, and everything will be fine." We gave each other a group hug, and Mom darted to her team.

In the stands, fans were packed like human watermelons, and people were standing all over the place in the 100-degree heat, but it was worth it. Within thirty minutes of play, Berta's team was up by two, and my Mom's team was struggling to get a grip on the game. One hour into the final, Mom and Berta squared off again, but Berta was too hot to stop, and in three fast pitches, Mom was out. When Berta's team was up to bat, Mom's team didn't let one player past first base.

There were only seven minutes left in the game when Mom's team came up to bat. They were down by two, but you could feel something was going to happen. The first batter, Virna, knocked the first pitch into left field, and made it to first base. The second batter, our mom, walked to home plate with a wall of cheers behind her. Berta stayed focused and burned the first pitch. "Strike!" Mom stepped back and regained her thoughts and raised her bat for the second pitch. Berta's second pitch was faster. "Strike two!" the umpire shouted. The fans went nuts with whistles and shouts.

Mom stepped back from the plate, adjusted her cap, got in the batter's box, and pointed to left field. The crowd let out an "Oooooooo." Berta took in a deep breath and fired another rocket, but this time Mom exploded the ball as promised. The crowd went crazy. Mom reached second base and Virna advanced to third base. You could see our father already giving orders to Virna about getting home.

Two minutes were left in the game, and the third batter, Delia, was always worth a hit. Berta tightened up and then threw like lightning, but Delia's bat was already in motion, and in a flash the ball went right back at Berta. The crowd let out a gasp as the ball hit Berta right in the face. Berta let out a loud cry, and the way she went down, you could tell she was hurt. Our father started shouting at Virna to run and Virna made it home. Our Mom ran through third and then slowed down and looked back at Berta and then ran to Berta. Our father went nuts, shouting, "What are you doing? Forget her!"

Mom knelt by Berta and helped her sit up, but our father kept shouting. The crowd fell silent, and all you could hear was our father screaming insults at our mother. Mom looked at our father, who was stomping and kicking dirt like a spoiled kid. Then she looked at us. We were in the dugout, and both of us were clutching the steel fence. We could tell she was asking us if it was OK to touch the ball. My sister's eyes began to water, and she turned to me and took my hand, and we nodded at Mom. We could see tears rolling down Mom's face, and she smiled at us. She slowly reached for the ball, and our father went ape crazy and started screaming, "Don't you dare touch that ball! Leave it alone."

Our Mom put her hand on the ball, clenched it, and picked it up. She raised it above her head for the world to see, and everyone held their breath. Then there was a break in the dark clouds and a ray of light embraced Tía Berta and Mom. And then Mom turned her hand and let the ball drop into the red dirt. The fans let out a sea of cheers that poured on the field and lifted Tía Berta and our mother. I looked at Rosana, and she turned to me and said softly, "Mom is the best," and it echoed through every ballpark in the world.

So Much for the Cubs

by Melissa Hidalgo

**Y DAD LEFT WITHOUT ME IN THE BOTTOM OF** the seventh. His slow but deliberate movements signaled to me that he was quietly pissed and at a loss for what to do. And not even a rare Cubs home game rife with every wonderful baseball cliché that played out in favor of his team was enough to keep him from committing true fan blasphemy at the most perfect baseball cathedral ever built. He left, and I let him go.

I had planned this for months. Bought the tickets back around Opening Day, in fact, right after Mom called to say that she and Dad were coming out to Chicago for a visit. I had been living in Chicago for nearly five years and attending ⌐⌐⌐ at Northwestern. I hated it and wondered ⌐ thick volumes of Victorian ⌐ something important to say ⌐. I wanted to travel. I wanted

⌐y studies despite the nagging ⌐ Mom called and told me she

and Dad were coming to visit, my mood lifted as I kicked right into baseball mode, flipping through the schedule to see if the Cubs were even playing at home the week my parents would be here. They were, and they were playing my L.A. Dodgers. Sweet serendipity! Dad had never seen a Cubs game at Wrigley Field, and I wanted to be the first one to take him. I bought the good seats, two of them, right above the third base line and the Cubs dugout. He wouldn't even need his binoculars.

The only other time Dad made it to Wrigley was when his unit sent him back to the Navy base just north of the city. It was during the off-season, and the most he could manage was a guided tour of that famed ballpark. Wrigley Field and the Cubs were the heart of Chicago, Dad always said, his words swollen with nostalgia for a place he never really knew. He'd been born in Joliet, Illinois, about fifty miles southwest of Chicago, but had never made it out to Wrigley Field.

When Dad was two, my grandfather moved the *familia* to Los Angeles to find work that did not involve steel mills or railroads. Los Angeles was the only city Dad ever knew. He bought Dodger season tickets and bled Lakers purple and gold, but he lived for the days when his Cubbies came to town to play the Dodgers, usually only once or twice every season, and usually losing to them.

Dad's L.A. upbringing never diluted his baseball loyalty to the Chicago Cubs. That team, with their storied history and mythical ballpark, tugged at Dad's heart and reminded him of a kind of home. As I grew older, I came to terms with it as a tortured love affair. The Cubs never won. As a child I thought it was just weird that Dad would break the rules as I saw them. Who goes to Dodger games—and has season tickets!—to root for the other team?

One year, I finally asked him: "Dad, how come you like the Cubs so much?" I was eight years old and couldn't understand why anybody who grew up in L.A. could root for any team besides the Dodgers.

He looked at me steadily and replied, "Because I was born in Chicago."

"No you weren't! Mom said you were born in Illinoise or something," I countered.

Dad laughed and said, "Chicago is in *Illinoy*. Not 'Illinoise.' I was born in a town near Chicago."

"So how come you don't like that team, from the place you were born?" I was a persistent kid who wanted answers.

"That town didn't have a team. The closest city with baseball was Chicago, so people liked the White Sox or the Cubs," he said.

"Oh. How come you don't like the White Sox then?"

He looked serious when he said, "The White Sox cheated a long time ago, and their ballpark is in a dangerous neighborhood. And they play in the American League." Then Dad pontificated about the evils of the designated hitter, words he spat out in disgust, like bad chew or rotten sunflower seeds.

"Oh." I took in the new baseball knowledge and thought about teams and home. "And I like the Dodgers because I was born here, right?" I was filling up with the youthful satisfaction of learning something new and important about baseball and my dad.

"That's right." Dad half-smiled and passed me the binoculars so I could watch Bill Russell, Steve Sax, and Steve Garvey turn a perfect 6-4-3 double play.

So I ordered the tickets for a game several weeks away, and memories of sweet summers spent with Dad at Dodger Stadium flooded my being. I was the tomboy daughter, the son he never had, Mom liked to say. Going to Dodgers games was our bonding time. We talked about everything, and the ballpark made it easy to say even the hardest things to him. Going to the games with Dad was especially liberating to me because it meant that it was okay for me to wear my cap, mitt, and jersey, and to look and act like a boy, and Dad wouldn't care because that's what you wore at ballgames. Except this one time, though, at a Dodgers game against the Cubs, when the concessions lady had asked him if his son would like a frozen malt with that Dodger dog. Dad's high-spirited countenance fell flat. "That's my daughter," he mumbled to the mortified hot dog lady. That was the only time Dad ever said anything about my short hair, and the only time I didn't wear my Dodgers cap the entire game. I was ten.

The phone rang and abruptly returned me to reality. It was Nena. "Hi, *papi*," she said to me. I loved it when she called me that. "How you doing? How's the work coming along?" she asked in her rapid-fire *Boriqua* style.

"Hi, babe," I said. I was distracted by baseball and thoughts of me and Dad at Wrigley watching the Cubs and

Dodgers duke it out. "Not much going on here. Haven't touched anything today," I said, flatly. "Mom kept me on the phone most of the morning. I got Cubs tickets, though."

"Oh, yeah? Who you taking?" Nena's voice hadn't changed yet, but it was on the verge.

"Don't worry, babe. They're for Dad when he comes out here. He's never been to a Cubs game," I said in my most matter-of-fact voice. "Besides," I continued, honey in my voice, "I'd rather go to a White Sox game with you anyway."

"Mmm-hmm," she replied, in her I'll-believe-it-when-I-see-it tone. "*¿Y tu mami?* How's she doing?"

"She's fine. I'm just worried about Dad as usual. She says hi to you, though," I tell Nena.

"*Hola, mami,*" Nena sings back as if Mom could hear her. "But what's up with your dad?"

"He's been in San Diego for a month now and I guess they can't decide if they're gonna ship him out to the Gulf or keep him stateside. But they're real excited about coming here to visit," I said.

"Ay, that sucks. I hope they figure their shit out. For your *Papi*'s sake, at least. The Navy's always doing some messed-up shit. Don't even get me started about Vieques—"

"*Ay,* Nena," was all I could muster.

"*Bueno,* the visit will be good," Nena said, encouragingly. Then she added, "Maybe you can talk with your dad about things."

"We'll see. I just want to enjoy the ballgame with him," I insisted.

"Alright, *papi*, we'll talk about it later. I gotta go get ready for work, but call me later, yeah?"

"Yeah, babe. Hey, wanna come over later?" I was relieved to avert a possibly unpleasant conversation through a sudden flush of desire for my beautiful Nena.

"Ay, I can't, *amor*, I'm sorry. I gotta work an extra shift tonight, but I can come over in the morning, wake you up real good," Nena's words cooed into my ear.

"I can't wait. Love you, baby."

I hung up the phone and daydreamed about Nena's lips and hips for a minute before getting back to my ridiculous stack of books and library materials. I came to realize that this whole academic game was bullshit. I was over the romanticized image of a life spent reading and writing great things. I spent the whole of the previous semester thinking that I had to get off my ass and do something, something else besides this. My mind zoomed back to baseball.

THE DAY OF THE BIG GAME AT WRIGLEY ARRIVED SOON AFTER MY parents did. I held the golden tickets in my hand like I was Charlie taking Grandpa to the chocolate factory. My face eased into a big smile and all my grad school troubles disappeared faster than a Sammy Sosa home run ball. That morning Dad and I dropped off Mom at the Miracle Mile to spend the day shopping and sightseeing. She was excited to see where Oprah taped her show.

"Have fun, *m'ija*," Mom said to me. "Bye, honey," she told Dad as she pecked him on the cheek. Then she whispered in my ear, "Talk to your father," before we parted.

I smiled and nodded as if she had said something sweet. She watched us and waved as Dad and I rushed to nearest train that would take us to Wrigley Field nice and early to watch batting practice. She knew the drill.

The buzz and excitement of game day was palpable. Nothing beats the majestic view of Wrigley Field's old-time neighborhood ballpark edifice unfolding before your eyes as you step off the train, that candy-red sign popping out to proudly announce, "Home of Chicago Cubs," to the world. The unmistakable whiff of a Cubs home game hits you as soon as the train doors open onto Addison Street. The smell of beer and burgers lingers together with the scents of sunscreen and too much bad men's cologne, whipped around by the Lake Michigan winds, even on a balmy summer day.

I watched Dad's face as we stepped off the train and made our way to the gate. He moved swiftly in his Ryne Sandberg jersey, circa 1988, and the brand-spankin'-new Cubs cap he had just bought at the first souvenir stand we saw. His trusty binoculars swung around his neck as he pumped his legs, faster, faster, as if rushing to the chow hall. I noticed how many Dodgers fans there were as we elbowed our way through the thick Cubs crowd, and I high-fived the other L.A. cap-wearing fans as we made our way to the stands.

Unpleasant questions invaded my otherwise blithe baseball state. Did he have any idea about what I wanted to talk about? Did Mom say anything to him yet? Maybe he's totally oblivious and I won't have to say anything to him today? Or maybe he already knows and I won't have to say anything to him today? I told myself to stop with the twenty questions and just enjoy the moment. Don't mess things up for Dad. It was his first Cubs home game for chrissakes.

We entered the stadium and Dad stopped, mouth agape, taking it all in. His eyes beheld the immaculate green of the turf. The crisp white pinstriped uniforms. The crack of the bat, the sounds of the players echoing from the field. The ivy growing on the outfield brick wall. Mark Grace. Andre Dawson. His favorite player, Ryne "Ryne-O" Sandberg. And I saw Dad's face turn up to the broadcast booth. He was looking for old Harry Caray, the venerable Cubs announcer, in all his silver-topped and bespectacled glory. Harry Caray was a baseball legend, like Tommy Lasorda or Vin Scully, and he made everyone want to root for the Cubbies.

"Holy cow," Dad said, echoing Harry Caray's famous expression. The words dripped from his mouth without irony as he savored the sights and sounds of Wrigley Field before him. This was heaven for him.

"Beautiful, yeah?" I said to Dad. I placed my hand on his shoulder as we made our way down to the field level seats near the Cubs dugout to see if we could shag a few balls during batting practice. Our gloved, outstretched hands stabbed at the air every time a ball came our way, even if it was way out of our reach. A Ryne Sandberg blooper miraculously found its way into Dad's glove. The ball was perfectly white except for a scuff of pine tar from the bat. A gift from the baseball gods. Dad held on to that ball for the entire game, the souvenir of a lifetime.

The game was a wild one, each team crossing the plate nine times before the seventh inning stretch. The Cubs' home crowd, mirthfully riled up as usual in the middle of the seventh, was on its feet as if it was the bottom of the ninth. Dad put his arm around me and swayed to the organ music during Harry Caray's famous seventh-inning serenade. "And it's root, root, root for the Cuuuuhh-bees," but I yelled out "DOD-GERS!" because I had to represent. Dad beamed and went nuts with the other Cubs fans after Harry's "whoa-yeah!" that always punctuated his rendition of "Take Me Out to the Ballgame."

Bottom of the seventh. My Dodgers went down in order, and now it was the Cubs' turn to bat. Dad sensed a win and was flush with excitement. Perhaps his cheap beer buzz emboldened him to chat me up about my life. *How's school? You gonna graduate soon? What's that thing you're working on again, that really long paper that's like a book?* He asked me twenty questions as he played with his prized Ryne Sandberg batting practice ball. I started to get a little nervous because the questions kept on coming like consecutive hits up the middle.

"Fine, Dad. Everything's fine." The Dodgers walked two in a row and Tommy Lasorda trotted to the mound. I decided it was time to get one more round before they stopped serving beer. I stood up and announced to Dad that I was going to get a beer, did he want anything. But when I took out my wallet and saw I only had a few bucks left, he handed me a twenty. "Thanks, Dad," I said and patted him on the shoulder before I hurried up the stairs.

I came back splashing beer from the giant tumblers to find that the Cubs had scored two runs with nobody out. When I got to our seats, I wondered why Dad was sitting down. He was inspecting something in his hand, a card or piece of paper. He sat still as all the other fans around him were cheering wildly. I sat next to Dad, held out his beer, but he didn't take it. Instead, he turned his head and looked at me with dark eyes.

"What's this?" he asked as he thrust the card at me. My face fell as my brain searched for answers. I grabbed my newly-minted Navy identification from him and shoved it in my pocket. "Nothing." I was trapped. I had to explain.

"You joined the *Navy*?" he asked, his question dripping with disgust, his face reddening, his dark eyes darting up and down my body as he searched for answers.

"No. I mean, I don't know. Delayed Entry Program. You know." I stumbled, suddenly ashamed that I even went so far as to enlist and possibly ship out for boot camp in six months.

Before I could say anything more, the stadium erupted in a deafening roar. I didn't notice that the Cubs had loaded the bases for a Mark Grace grand slam. My father sat oblivious.

I saw Dad's mouth move as he spat out mean words to my face, his heated voice rising above the crowd. I sat motionless, staring at the blur of the ballgame and losing myself in the cacophony of claps, cheers, and whistles.

I finally mustered up the *ganas* to talk back. "I thought you'd be happy. I'm sick of grad school. Mom says she's fine with it." I lied to my dad to see what he said, on the verge of tears.

The inning was a Dodgers' disaster. I couldn't watch anymore, but I was stuck to my seat. My father, ignoring the Cubs' show of baseball force, began to gather his things.

He turned to me. "What does your *girlfriend* think about this?" He sneered when he said the word "girlfriend."

My eyes widened. He knew about Nena? "They don't like your kind, you know," he stated, as if daring me. His face softened as he realized his unfatherly manner, and he looked at me with sadness and disappointment. Binoculars in one hand, his prized Sandberg batting practice ball in the other, he gave the order: "Let's go."

"You go." I was pissed as I waited to see how long this game would last. Then the daughter in me, the ten-year-old tomboy in me, really wanted to just watch the ballgame with her father. I pleaded, "C'mon, Dad. Let's just watch the game." He slung his binoculars around his neck and took the Sandberg ball in his giant, soft hand. He rolled it around, inspecting it closely. Dejected, he handed me the ball, pivoted with military precision, and kicked his beer over as he walked away.

I stared at Dad as he disappeared up the stairs and into the swarm of fans, and my heart sank as I held the heavy ball in my hand that no longer seemed special. It looked like just another scuffed baseball, a million just like it.

I watched the rest of the game in a dreamlike state, numb and alone, until the Cubs beat the Dodgers, who went down without a fight in the ninth inning. 1-2-3, easy outs, game over. I peeled myself off the seat. My legs felt like bags of sand as I climbed up the stairs begrudgingly. I caught Dad sitting in another seat, all by himself, at the far end of the section. He hung over the seat in front of him like dugout benchwarmers over the railings, witnessing their defeat. Not even a resounding Cubs victory here at Wrigley Field could muster up life in my father. His eyes met mine as I walked slowly over to him. He stood up, squared his shoulders, and left, the glory of a Cubs home victory lost in the accidental discovery of a Navy ID card. Though we walked within arm's reach of each other, he felt as far away as dead center field. Not a word passed between us as we marched out of the stands.

The Noble Roman
by Pete Cava

INSIDE THE CHALK-LINED BATTER'S BOX, HIS HEAD POUND-ing, side throbbing, knees aching, and one hit from immortality, Roman Cruz tired of waiting and signaled for time. Coming out of his crouch behind the New York catcher, the blue-clad umpire yanked up both hands like a man trying to stop traffic. Along with the crowd on hand for this final day of the regular season, the home plate ump was caught up in the drama unfolding before him.

With no score and two outs in the top of the ninth, in a meaningless contest between also-rans, Cruz was pinch-hitting for Chicago's pitcher. Roman Cruz—the Noble Roman—had batted safely two-thousand, nine-hundred ninety-nine times. A hit on this chilly, sunless Sunday afternoon would guarantee membership in a hallowed baseball circle and a Hall of Fame plaque.

New York's pitcher was a tall, rail-thin right-hander with ~olor of *cafecito*. The kid was a September call-up, ~or league debut. Venezuelan, maybe. Or ~or maybe Dominican?

Cordero. That was the kid's name, and he was mixing a slider in with his fastball and a curve that seemed to drop off a table. So far today, Cordero had retired twenty-six consecutive Chicago batters. If the kid retired Cruz, he would have a perfect game in his first outing. It had never happened in the big leagues.

Wiping a sweaty palm across the red letters on his gray jersey, Cruz shifted back into the batter's box. The noise from the crowd sounded like the roar of a jet engine. In the stands, the fans were nearly beyond restraint. In both dugouts the players were on their feet, screaming.

FOR THE PAST NINETEEN YEARS IN CHICAGO, ROMAN CRUZ HAD played baseball in a state of grace—three batting titles, two most valuable player awards, six Gold Gloves, and an arm like a rifle in right field. But Roman was now forty-one, plagued by rib and knee injuries. He'd been dogged by headaches since a late August game on the Coast, when a fastball had split his batting helmet. A career .316 hitter, his average had spiraled downward the past few seasons – .271 two summers ago, .253 last season. This year it hadn't risen above .230.

Cruz wasn't supposed to play. After Roman's last hit, Chicago manager Guy Rucker heard from the team owner: *Cruz sits for the rest of the season.* Chicago's first game next year was at home. Roman Cruz's quest for three-thousand hits would give ticket sales a healthy boost. There was all winter to build the hype. If the commissioner complained about holding out Cruz for the rest of this season, the club could always cite concerns for Roman's health.

But Chicago had eighty-one victories and eighty losses. A win today would guarantee a winning season, something Guy Rucker wanted badly. The grapevine said that once Roman Cruz got his three-thousandth hit, he was finished as a player. But Rucker's contract was up at the end of the year, and he would need all the ammunition he could get during contract negotiations. The last two years, Rucker's teams had fared even worse than Cruz's batting average. And the Chicago players, including Cruz, knew their manager would bowl over his own mother if it was to his advantage.

His face grim and mottled, Rucker stood at the edge of the dugout. His dark eyes went from Cruz to the New York pitcher and back to Cruz. Rucker knew Cruz's legend had outlived his skill. If the next hit was to be Cruz's last, this was an opportune time. And he was still the Noble Roman, a favorite of fans throughout the league.

And when the public address system crackled, "Batting for McCarty...number twenty-five... Roe-MAHN..." the fans exploded before the announcer could finish, sensing an epic confrontation.

SLOWLY WAVING HIS BAT, ROMAN CRUZ CLOSELY OBSERVED Cordero as the lanky pitcher peered in for the sign. Cordero was shaking off his catcher a second time when Cruz noticed a silver cross dangling from a chain around the kid's neck. As Cordero reached the set position, Cruz's body tensed. His eyes met Cordero's.

Roman thought he saw Cordero nod ever so slightly, thought he saw a slight smile as the pitcher went into his windup. The kid was one out away from the greatest pitching performance ever. And Roman Cruz knew he would throw a fastball.

The baseball sped toward the heart of home plate, a perfect offering. Cruz whipped around, got his hips into it, felt the bat meet the ball, heard the crack. For a moment there was silence. No one moved until Ballard, the New York right fielder, bolted suddenly toward the right field corner. A full body length from the bright yellow foul pole, Ballard leaped. The ball carried just beyond his glove to the other side of the short green wall, and landed in the midst of a roiling scrum of humanity on the other side.

Roman Cruz's three-thousandth career hit was a home run. Cordero's chance for a perfect game was over. And when the skinny New York pitcher struck out the next batter, Guy Rucker's club took a 1-0 lead into the bottom of the ninth.

CRUZ REMAINED IN THE GAME, TROTTING OUT TO REPLACE Schilling in right field. Clair came in to pitch for Chicago as part of a double switch. Barnett, New York's first batter, worked Clair for a walk. The next man grounded to third for the first out while the speedy Barnett took second. Clair fanned Heininger for the second out, bringing Wynalda, New York's clean-up hitter, to the plate. Clair's first two pitches were low and away. In right field, Roman Cruz tugged at the leather string on his glove and considered the possibilities: *Anything hit to me, get it home or we're tied up.*

Clair's next pitch was up and in. Wynalda whacked the ball into right-center field. Barnett, off with the crack of the bat, was around third and flying toward home plate when Cruz caught up to the baseball. In one fluid movement, Roman scooped up the ball and fired it to Perona, who had tossed aside his catcher's mask and was blocking the plate. The Noble Roman's throw was a strike. Barnett was out by three feet.

GENE VERDE HAD SKIPPED AFTERNOON CLASSES AT PELHAM University to cover the game for the National Press Agency. Before bolting out of the press box for the Chicago clubhouse, Verde scribbled down the numbers for Cordero, the rookie New York pitcher. Twenty-eight batters—one over the minimum—no walks, one hit, one run. And the loss.

At Cruz's locker, newspaper, radio and television reporters elbowed one another, shouting the same questions simultaneously. The cramped clubhouse reeked of sweat and wintergreen oil, mingled with the smell of the beer that Roman's teammates had sprayed over him in celebration. Cruz's coffee-with-cream complexion glistened as he tried to answer the avalanche of questions. A man of average height, Roman Cruz's face was strong-boned, if a trifle thin. The accent of his birthplace tinged his words.

Cruz said he knew that the New York pitcher—what's his name? Cordero? Yeah, Roman was aware that Cordero was one out away from a perfect game. Cruz said he was looking for a fastball, and he'd guessed right. Roman said nothing about the kid's barely perceptible smile, nothing about that slight nod.

Yeah, he felt bad for Cordero, Cruz said. It's tough to pitch a game like that and lose. But that's baseball, no? Besides, with the kind of stuff Cordero showed today, the kid might pitch ten perfect games before he's finished. The reporters laughed. That kid was good out there today, said Roman. Real good. And he had his whole career ahead of him. When Cruz reminded the reporters he was old enough to be Cordero's father, they laughed again.

The throw Cruz made to nail Barnett at the plate? Roman looked around the clubhouse. He forced his mouth into a grin. Crooking his right arm, Cruz flexed his muscle and said: *Still got it, guys,* and the reporters laughed some more.

Sure, it felt great to have three-thousand hits, said Cruz without emotion. *But where is the joy?* His ticket to Cooperstown had been punched, he thought, wishing the questions would stop coming. *Boxed in again.* At home plate, at least he'd been able to ask for time. *But not in here.*

Jotting down Cruz's words, Gene Verde began to think about a lead: *Roman Cruz stroked his three-thousandth career hit Sunday, a ninth-inning home run that gave visiting Chicago to a 1-0 win over New York. Cruz's blast spoiled the major league debut of rookie right-hander Javier Cordero, who was within one out of a perfect game when Cruz entered the game as a pinch-hitter.*

Verde noticed Cruz's odd detachment and considered his next paragraph. *Afterwards, answering reporters' questions at his locker, Cruz appeared discontented, like someone yearning for something elusive that will remain beyond his grasp forever.* But Verde knew that no wire service editor would let this through.

One by one the reporters began stealing away to the New York clubhouse to talk to Cordero. Verde was the last to leave. He and Cordero were about the same age, and Gene, too, had questions for the slender pitcher. Before Cruz's home run, Gene thought he'd seen Cordero nod his head and smile, ever so slightly.

But by the time Verde reached the New York clubhouse, Cordero had dressed and departed. The other reporters were back in the press box, typing stories.

ROMAN CRUZ SPENT THAT AUTUMN IN CHICAGO AND WAITED, still dogged by headaches, sore ribs and achy knees. Thanksgiving came and went, and Cruz heard nothing from the Chicago front office. The first week of December, there was a call from a reporter covering baseball's winter meetings. Guy Rucker had been given a one-year contract extension, based on Chicago's winning record. The owner had seen it as a sign of hope.

Rucker had told the reporter that Cruz would not be back as an active player. Instead, Rucker planned to go with a youth movement. Roman would be offered a coaching post with a minor league team.

ONE GRAY JANUARY MORNING, ROMAN CRUZ SPRAWLED ON THE couch in his Chicago apartment. He lingered over a cup of coffee, thinking about what a long road it had been. As a boy, he'd played baseball every day on the beach near his family's humble board-and-palm leaf *bohio* on the outskirts of the island nation's capital. Roman and the other boys played barefoot. Their bats were made from old broom handles, their gloves fashioned from cardboard. The ball they used was held together by tape. A pile of shells served as home plate. During every game the boys acted out a passion play, whooping at each pitch, jumping up and down like happy lunatics with each hit or catch. Roman had never again knew such pure joy. He loved the game. He wanted to go north to play in the *grandes ligas*, the big leagues.

By age twelve, Roman was hitting baseballs farther than the older boys. One day he drove a ball over a seawall into the bright blue waves. He rounded the bases as his teammates cheered, and Roman prayed the ball would travel all the way across the straits. All the way to the land of the *grandes ligas*, where a scout would find the ball and know that it was Roman Cruz who had hit it. And the scout would come to the *bohio* of the Cruz family, a contract in his hand.

Roman recited this prayer every day to the Virgin. In those days he had worn a silver cross, like the one Roman had spotted hanging from the chain around the neck of Cordero, the rookie New York pitcher. And when a scout finally did come with a contract, Roman Cruz quickly signed. He went off to play the game with real baseballs, real bats, and uniforms that looked like they were made for kings. He played in strange, cold cities where the greatest joy was winning and moving closer to the *grandes ligas*. The silver cross he left behind in his family's *bohio*. No longer did he pray to the Virgin.

Roman Cruz met Guy Rucker when they were teenagers playing in the minor leagues. Rucker was a third baseman and a good hitter. Cruz was known for his batting skills and his powerful right arm. Every day, Roman practiced throwing from right field to home plate. Opposing players soon quickly learned that to challenge him was a mistake.

Rucker and Cruz moved up the ladder together, arriving in Chicago the same year. They were opposites. Reporters dubbed Cruz the Noble Roman because of his reserved but dignified manner. The combative Rucker, writers agreed, had a clenched personality. Cruz and Rucker played together, roomed together on the road, and after the games they hit the bars together. There were always women. A teammate used to say that if he couldn't find a girl, he could always pick up whoever Rucker or Cruz rejected.

After years of the daily grind of professional sports, the glory faded. The booze didn't make Roman feel good any more. The women began to look alike. *Is this it,* he began to wonder? *This is all there is to it?*

The first to see his skills erode was Guy Rucker. At thirty-five his playing days were over. By then Chicago's manager, Old Doc Warner, was ready to retire and the Chicago owner thought the best man to replace him was the feisty Rucker. Cruz and Rucker no longer went out drinking. When Rucker went out with the ladies, Cruz no longer went along.

Managers room alone, so Rucker and Cruz drew further apart. After Roman's abilities started to diminish, the distance between them widened.

HE WAS NO LONGER A STAR, NOT EVEN AN EVERYDAY PLAYER, and Roman Cruz knew this. If he played again, it would be with another team. A pinch-hitter maybe, or perhaps as a player-coach. There would be no offers to manage, none for doing color commentary on radio or television. Not for a man with an accent and brown skin.

Cruz was still waiting by mid-February, when pitchers and catchers began reporting for spring training. In the sports pages he read about Cordero. The lean right-hander with the unhittable assortment of pitches had been playing in the winter leagues when his arm went bad.

THE SEASON STARTED, AND SOON IT WAS MIDSUMMER. Roman's side and knees were still sore, and sometimes the headaches returned. The only offer that had come his way was from Chicago, which wanted him to coach young players in a backwater town in the low minor leagues. He knew he was finished with baseball, or maybe it was the other way around.

There was nothing more for Roman Cruz in Chicago. He had put off marriage and a family until his playing days were over. But now that he was no longer a big league star, there were no prospects. There was no going back to his homeland. His family was all gone now. Roman looked back on his nineteen years in Chicago, his batting titles, the

MVP awards, the final hit that ensured him a place in the Hall of Fame. *So this is it.*

Cruz once again saw Cordero nod to him from the mound, again saw the skinny pitcher smile at him. He remembered what it was like when his bat connected with the baseball, the sound it made, and how it made Roman feel like he would live forever.

And Roman began to comprehend what Cordero had given him, and what must be done with it.

THE FIRST ANNIVERSARY OF ROMAN CRUZ'S LAST HIT WAS approaching when the hurricane ploughed through the Caribbean. When a second storm hit two days later, the largest island in the West Indies lay in ruins. Crops in the country's western half were ruined. There was no electricity and no running water.

Even though Roman Cruz's adopted country no longer had political ties to the island nation, he didn't wait. Cruz's calls for a relief effort made the papers, made network news. In the sports column he wrote for his college newspaper, Gene Verde proclaimed Cruz's efforts greater than any of the Noble Roman's three-thousand hits. Greater than his outfield skills. Greater than his powerful throwing arm.

THE FIRST FINANCIAL CONTRIBUTION CAME FROM THE OWNER OF the Chicago team. Perhaps out of guilt, or possibly, because it would get Roman Cruz away from Chicago. The club was in last place. Roman's presence was a reminder that the team's youth movement had been a failure.

A smaller donation from Guy Rucker followed, along with a public endorsement. Guy knew his days as manager were numbered. If he was to get another job in baseball, Rucker needed some good ink.

ROMAN CRUZ WAS ABOARD THE CHARTERED FLIGHT THAT landed on the stricken island with the first shipment of supplies. The cargo plane landed in one of the badly-run dictatorship's eastern cities. Local government officials mustered a caravan of creaking military vehicles to carry the bottled water, canned foods, and clothing from east to west. Riding in a covered jeep at the head of the column, Cruz perspired in the oppressive heat and humidity, but he was glad to be out of the searing tropical sun. At least the headaches had stopped, and the pains in his side and his knees had subsided.

The relief convoy passed through the mountainous inland region, where three bodies of water converged in the wilderness. As they meandered along the swollen river, the driver of the jeep explained that the closest civilization was a monastery that dated back to colonial days. The monastery's inhabitants were isolated and self-sufficient, so the government, officially atheist, left them alone.

The first two bridges they came across had been washed out by the floodwaters. The third they found was a rarely used wood-and-steel relic with triangular trusses on each side of its three-hundred meter span. *We go first*, Roman told the driver of the jeep, *and the others will follow*.

The jeep had passed the midpoint and was about seventy meters from the opposite bank when the bridge began to give way. A shriek of grinding metal filled the air, followed by a fusillade of splintering beams. Slowly, the disintegrating bridge began to slide into the torrent.

The jeep driver jumped first. Cruz leaped as the trusses on his side of the span pulled apart. He didn't see the length of rotting timber until just before it smashed his face. Roman's last thoughts were about the water that closed over him.

RESCUERS FOUND THE DRIVER OF THE JEEP DOWNSTREAM, WET, shivering and frightened, but still alive. There was no sign of Roman Cruz. His corpse was never recovered.

Cruz's fate was the lead story for days. The owner of the Chicago team announced that next year his players would wear black armbands in memory of the Noble Roman. A month later the owner announced that Guy Rucker would not be retained as manager.

The following year on opening day, major-league clubs observed a moment of silence in memory of Roman Cruz. The pre-game memorial service in Chicago was broadcast around the Caribbean.

Javier Cordero watched it at his home. Cordero's sore arm had never come around. He would never pitch again.

SURROUNDED BY VOLUMES AND WOULD-BE BOOKS IN HIS NEW York office, Penniston Byrnes scanned the letter that accompanied the manuscript. Penn recognized Gene

Verde's by-line from the sports pages, and from previous books with rival publishers.

Penn Byrnes remembered Roman Cruz, the baseball Hall of Famer. *How many years has it been?* Penn found the answer in Gene's query letter: twenty-five years this summer.

The letter mentioned Javier Cordero, the pitcher who came within an out of perfection in his only major league game, only to see it end when Cruz stroked his three-thousandth and final hit.

After his arm went lame, Cordero had gone back to his home country. He'd opened a baseball instructional school for young players. Today Cordero scrounged support from wherever he could find it. Verde wanted half of any royalties to go to Cordero's baseball school.

Verde's letter included quotes from an interview with Cordero. Yes, he'd come close to perfection, said Cordero. But there were no regrets. Roman Cruz had inspired him and many others, so many others. Cordero was content to be remembered as the pitcher who gave up Cruz's last hit. He was the Noble Roman, Cordero said, and he played the game in a state of grace. And at the end, that was how Roman Cruz lived his life.

Penniston Byrnes scanned Gene's proposal a second time and decided to take no immediate action. Roman Cruz is still a recognizable name, and Verde's book, *The Noble Roman*, might sell. But, Penn wondered: How do you arrange a book tour for a dead Spic?

THE CHURCH OF NUESTRA SEÑORA DEL CARMEN LAY IN THE poorest part of the grim regime's third-largest city. Religion was flourishing, with the government's uneasy tolerance.

A tan mongrel cantered out of the church, pursued by an Old Man with a patch over his right eye. A small silver cross dangled from the chain around his neck.

The boys sat in the back of the church, gloves and caps beside them in the pews. They glanced back at the sideshow as white-haired Padre Andrés recited the Eucharistic Prayer: *...but by rising from the dead, he destroyed death and restored life. And that we might live no longer for ourselves but for his.*

The boys were restless, but Padre Andres and the Old Man insisted they attend morning service on days when they practiced or played a game. And today the boys were playing for the city championship.

...From age to age you gather a people to yourself, so that from East to West a perfect offering may be made to the glory of your name.

Padre Andrés said the Old Man came from the mountains, where he'd lived in the old monastery with the monks for many years. After the monks had died out, the Old Man had come down the mountain to the city. He had asked Padre Andrés for meals and a place to sleep in return for odd jobs.

The Old Man was tough to look at, with a scar that streaked out from under his black eye patch. The rest of his face was like the reflection in a broken mirror.

...Lord, may this sacrifice, which has made our peace with you, advance the peace and salvation of all the world.

The Old Man worked with the baseball team of *Nuestra Señora Del Carmen* Church. The boys wanted badly to win the championship today. They wanted to win for the Old Man, because they loved him. He taught them to play with joy. He told them to play like he knew they could, to play—how did the Old Man always put it?—to play like they are in a state of grace.

And after the game, if the boys were victorious, the Old Man would trot out to right field like always after they won, and he would celebrate by making that long, perfect throw to home plate.

...Through him, with him, in him, in the unity of the Holy Spirit, all glory and honor is yours, almighty Father, forever and ever. Amen.

As the boys filed up the aisle for Communion, the Old Man walked with them.

The Heat

by Thomas de la Cruz

**N THE LAST SATURDAY OF THE MONTH, OUR** church celebrated birthdays. Usually we had a picnic in some park, or lunch after the service, but one month my father suggested we have a barbecue at our house. During which the church's youth team would have a friendly baseball game across the street on the empty lots that had become the diamond. They used to be *montes* until we cleaned them. A large mesquite still stands in right field, but no one hits it that way, so it doesn't really matter. We didn't know who the land belongs to, but no one told us anything so we just kept clearing the field. The ground wasn't leveled, though and sometimes we'd twist our ankles on a hole or trip over a hidden rock. My father said it made us better players. "Nothing tests your reflexes like a grounder on an uneven field."

Mr. Villarreal was the deacon of the church, and the unofficial cook. When he pulled into the driveway that Saturday I helped him carry the charcoal to the pit.

"I remember when your dad played, *m'ijo*. We'd call him 'The Heat' because *tenía un brazo*."

"You saw him play?"

"Ooohh. Years ago. When we were still young." Mr. Villarreal smiled at me as he poured the charcoal into the barbeque pit. "Don Hermán was the best. *Puro* strike down the middle."

Many people told me about "The Heat," but I had never seen my father play. He coached both the children's team, and the youth team for our church. My two older brothers played for the youth team, so I got to see their games. They never lost. I had to play for the children's team, though. We lost all the time.

"On the days when it'd be too hot to work in the fields your dad would still manage to get us on the diamond. *Estábamos locos* back then."

"Why don't you play anymore?"

"Ay, I ran out of fire. *Te imaginas,* your dad and I used to work ten hour shifts in the fields. Bent over, or dragging hundred pound sacks of cotton. Taking salt pills so we wouldn't pass out from the heat."

"Ten hours?"

"*Diez horas, m'ijo*. I can't play anymore. If I were to swing the bat, *n'ombre*, I'll break something. But watching you guys run out there makes me remember."

I helped Mr. Villarreal pour the last bit of charcoal into the pit when Noel, my oldest brother, walked up to me. "You want to play today?"

Mr. Villarreal caught the bag of charcoal as it slipped out of my hands. He laughed, and turned to Noel, "I think that's a yes."

An absolute yes. I had never been invited to play with them before, but he also had a habit of torturing me, though. Do you want ice cream? Yes. Well so do people in hell. Do you want to go to the movies? Yes. Well so do people in prison. Do you want the elastic from your underwear back? If you wouldn't mind. Well, so do nerds all around the world. But the chance to play on the youth team was worth the risk, so I answered a cautious "yes." To my relief he nodded his head and walked away.

Mr. Villarreal motioned for me to step back as he soaked the charcoal with lighter fluid. "Noel turned out just like your dad too. *Pero ese*," he whistled, and pointed off into the distance, "he destroys the baseball, *m'ijo*."

I had seen how the infield backed up when Noel stepped to the plate, and the outfielders got as close to the fence as possible. He had no mercy, and never struck out. "My cousin can strike you out, Noel. He plays for the leagues in Mexico." Well bring him. And sure enough a week later they'd come. Full of confidence and certainty. I, along with the rest of the neighborhood kids, stood in awe as Noel took the plate. I'd study his form closely from the moment he picked up the bat. They'd come from all around the Valley, full of confidence, and certainty only to leave with disappointment.

"They're starting to warm up, *mira*" Mr. Villarreal pointed towards the field where the players were beginning to show up, "I can take care of things here. *Vete, órale.*"

I ran towards the field to ensure I got there before they'd somehow start, and forget that I'd been invited.

"Save it for the game," Noel said as I came up next to him breathing hard and placing my palms on my knees.

"He's playing?" I looked up to see my other brother, Hermán, walking towards us. We didn't call him junior, and to solve any confusion we said his name in English. "We playing little league or what?"

I curled my toes making the top of my shoes rise. Officially, Noel was team captain, but unofficially "Herman" didn't care. Both of them held their own position of leadership. If he said that I couldn't play then I'd be watching the game.

"He's playing," Noel said as he handed me a glove. "Dad's playing too."

Herman cocked his head slightly back, and he stopped walking towards us. "Ah, OK," he said, then looked at Noel for a moment and nodded once.

"Dad's playing?" I asked to make sure I had heard right.

"Yup."

"Today?"

Noel looked at me, squinted his eyes, and then walked away. My father was playing. The Heat was taking the pitcher's mound on the same day I was asked to play. My father was coming out of retirement, and I had front row seats to his return. This was too much. Everyone talked about The Heat, but I had never seen him. During practice he'd hit the ball to us and sometimes tossed it back when we'd fail to catch it, but that was about it. I put on my glove and looked around for my father. I had seen him earlier, but for some reason I expected to find him in uniform with his pant legs tucked into his knee high socks. Two red strips at the top of them with a baseball cap in his back pocket.

"Go warm up with him." Herman pointed towards the pitcher's mound where my father stood, dressed in khaki pants and a faded polo shirt, no knee-high socks, no number on his back. "And take this."

I looked at what Hermán held in his hands, and instantly recoiled. The regulation softball promised that I wouldn't be fully accepted into the big leagues. "Are we out of baseballs?"

"No."

"Then."

"Then what?"

"Why are we going to play with the softball?"

"Because you're a little punk and you'll get hurt and cry to mom, and she'll say 'Hermán, why did you let Pete play with the hardball?' And I'll say, 'Because he's a little punk and didn't want to take the softball,' and she'll say—"

"But I won't get hurt. I can play baseball. I can—"

He threw the ball at my chest forcing me to catch it. "Soft ball or no ball. You decide."

I was a lot younger than my two older brothers, and they would tell me that I was an accident, because my parents had them two years apart, and then they waited fifteen years to have me. My father had just turned forty-eight. I asked my mother once after my brothers had made me cry if I was an accident. She looked at me in the most endearing of ways and placed her hand on my head, *"M'ijo,* you were all accidents." So I didn't feel bad about it anymore except my brothers constantly excluded me from their activities because I was too small. But if the team had two captains it only had one general. My father could get them to change their minds.

"*M'ijo,* you're small. It's better we play with the softball."

"But you've seen me play. You don't think I can play fastball?"

"I know you can, but these guys hit hard."

"But if you pitch with the hardball then they won't get a chance to hit it, right?"

"That's right." He smiled at me and tapped my chest with this glove. "But I've played hardball all my life, *m'ijo.* I don't mind taking a break."

"But I haven't seen you pitch and you're going to use a softball?"

"The hardball moves faster than the soft one, and sometimes it's harder to see."

"But I'll be careful."

"Pete, it can do a lot of damage if it hits you, so we're playing with the soft one. Now, *órale,* get back and warm up with me." At least I was playing with the youth team. None of the kids I played with till then knew what that felt like. "You don't have to get so far," my father told me while I walked away from him. "We're just warming up. *Vente,* get closer."

"But everyone else is further. Look."

"Don't worry about them. You worry about the heat, *mira.*" He then stood in pitcher position, slightly leaned over, legs apart, right hand behind his back holding the ball while his fingers toyed with it.

"The heat?" Finally. I squatted down and placed my glove at the strike zone.

"Okay, m'ijo. Puro strike."

I placed my free hand between my thighs and started with the fastball, one finger down. "Let's see it. Órale, the heat." But he only shook his head. Okay then. I put down two fingers, hit my glove, and began yelling, "Let's go. Fire the cannon. Órale, the heat." Still, he kept shaking his head. Three fingers down? The slow pitch. "I'm cold, apá. I need some heat.

"We need to warm up," he said and waited till I gave the correct signal. I looked around to see the rest of the team already fifty feet apart, and trying to break each other's hands. "Don't worry about them. You worry about the heat."

I gave him the signal for the slow ball. Three fingers down. I braced myself, because I expected it to hurt, but it didn't knock me back. It didn't even sting my hand.

"Puro strike. Did you see? Right down the middle."

"What strike? You pitched it so slow that the batter hit it out of the park. I can take a fast pitch, you don't have to go easy on me." Then I stood up, and threw it so hard that I stumbled forward. I didn't see the ball hit my father's glove, but I heard the impact. When I looked up my dad had taken off his glove.

"Throw out your arm by yourself if you want," he said while floating the ball to my feet and walking towards the pitcher's mound.

Is he saving his arm for the game? But he's pitching underhand. I should've let him warm up. He would have thrown it harder. But he's probably saving it for the game. No way he'll only pitch underhand. No way. Maybe the last innings when he's warmed up. I spent the next few minutes throwing the ball into the air, and catching it on the way down.

After everyone warmed up the two team captains, Noel and Hermán, began choosing their players. My father announced he would pitch for both teams, and walked to the plate. I wanted to ask why, but I was too busy not getting picked that I ignored it. I stood at the line, and with every chosen player felt less excited to be included in the game. I didn't get picked last, though, Santos did, but he is left handed, and we didn't have any lefty gloves.

"You're playing short stop." My brother told me as we took the field.

"Shortstop? But that's where you play."

"Well, today that's where you play." My brother argued that shortstop takes care of the team. "That's why I play shortstop," he'd always say. "I carry the team."

After practically being chosen last he still had enough confidence in me to let me play shortstop. Had he seen me playing on the children's team? Did my father tell him about the double play I did last week? Was this a test to see if it was time to move up? I felt excited, but I knew something was off though. On the day my father plays not only am I allowed to join, but Noel gives up his spot. I looked around waited for someone to slap me in the back of the head. *We're just messing with you punk. Now get off the field. Hey look, everyone. He really thought we'd let him play. Oh how silly of him to think that.*

I waited for the hidden cameras, and the barrage of laughter. Nothing, though. Herman picked his lineup, and Noel stretched in right field. They really did intend to let me play.

"A little more to your left, little guy." Third basemen Leo smiled at me as he signaled with his glove to move closer to second base. "That way we can cover this whole section."

Leo lived in the corner house with his mother who yelled at us every morning while we waited for the bus. Most of the time she'd yell at the trees and power lines, but one time I lifted the flag on her mailbox, and she yelled at me until the bus drove away. Leo came to my house that day and apologized, but I told him it was my fault. He told me not to worry about it, and not to be scared the next day. "She forgets things," he said.

"Nothing's gonna pass through here, Leo."

"That's right, Pete."

He gave me the thumbs up, and disarmed me of the paranoia I had been feeling. My father pointed at me before pitching, and I nodded my head. I got close to the ground and waited anxiously. Then my brother yelled something from center field loud enough for everyone to hear. It echoed through the air, and I heard it fade into the distance. "Peter's playing the infield," he said. "Don't hit it hard."

Is this why he had asked me to play shortshop? So he could make fun of me in front of the whole team? As my older brother I expected a certain amount of torture, but this new kind of cruelty didn't make sense. He'd never embarrassed me before in front of so many people. The ladies from the church turned away from each other, looked in my direction, and whispered what I could only imagine were prayers they thought I'd need. The rest of the infield started laughing and making comments. *If the ball come towards you too fast you can always hide behind me. Just close your eyes, and put your glove in front of you.* Cover your *huevos, man, or you'll never have kids.* Leo called my name softly and told me not to listen, but even his kind words annoyed me.

"Hit it as hard as you want. I play better than everyone on this team combined. Noel you can kiss my—"

"Pete, that's enough." I stood silently and stared at my father while the rest of the team smiled.

Then he winked at me. "Ready?"

I remained quiet, but Leo spoke up, "He's ready, Don Hermán. Come on, Pete. You and me."

I saw his kind eyes even behind the pitch black of his sunglasses. "All right, Leo. You and me."

Noel yelled once more from center field not to hit it hard, but this time he didn't blame it on me. My father wound up as if he intended to fast ball it down the middle of the plate, but at the last moment floated the ball underhand towards the strike zone. Slow enough for the guy holding the bat to count the red stitches on the ball. *Always assume the ball will be hit towards you, Pete. Stay low to the ground. Loosen up.* By the time the ball made contact with the bat I was already on my toes.

The three outs came quickly. Two caught by the outfielders, and a grounder to third. Leo didn't have any trouble getting to it and laughed as the runner stopped halfway to first base.

"Why are you stopping? *Córrele*, Charlie." Even if the ball crawled towards first and jumped into the glove, my father still expected everyone to at least try to make it. *People make mistakes, so don't stop until you're sure you're out*. That went for pop-flies too. In Charlie's defense, though, Leo hardly made any mistakes, so I wouldn't have bothered either.

I left my glove on the floor where I stood, as did the rest of the team, and made my way off of the field. My brother picked the lineup, and I landed last to bat. *We need to get people on base. At the end you'll bring them home. We don't want easy outs.* Their excuses didn't bother me as much as the thought of my father pitching underhand. No one else seemed to care, but I had always been pitched underhand. I stood with the big boys, so everyone got the child treatment.

I felt guilty, because we could hit the ball as hard as we wanted. They didn't have a twelve-year-old on their team. I figured Hermán would've said something, but he whistled all the way to center field. It must have been understood, though, that we wouldn't hit it hard either because third baseman Leo, who hits almost as hard as Noel, simply tapped it over second base. The next two after him also hit it softly. Hermán had said it best. We were playing little league because of me. With every weak hit I tightened my grip around the bat. White knuckles and red palms promised a punishing end to this little league game. Every time the softball floated towards home plate I imagined myself smashing its face in and sending it whirling towards my house. Past Villarreal who fanned the charcoal, over the ladies from the church, barely missing my brother's glove and leaving my father behind.

By the time they managed to get two outs on us we were up by three and had two runners on base. In my still building anger I almost didn't notice as Noel took the bat from me. "I think I'll use this light one today." He stepped up to the plate, and pointed to the ladies from the church. "Hey!" he yelled. "Cover your heads!" The shouting immediately followed from our cheerleaders. I had never seen him do this. It was like he wanted everyone to see him hit a ball off of The Heat. My father has to pitch it overhand now. *Noel is going to destroy that softball. He has to do it.*

My father waved the ladies off and turned to my brother. "Puro strike, Noel."

"I'm gonna have to buy you a new window for the house, *apá*."

"*Vamos a ver.*" My father's smile went away, and he moved his glove closer to his face exposing only his eyes from in between the cap visor, and the top of the glove. Like a knight who intended to drop his opponent from his horse he stood in silence. Villarreal turned away from the now sizzling fajita and took a few steps closer to the field. The ladies still talked but no longer looked at one another. Noel planted his feet and drew back his bat like a swordsman.

Everyone grew about two inches when my father picked up his left leg, and in one graceful motion brought it down while moving his left arm forward like a ballet dancer about to backhand someone in the face. His right arm drew back, and at the last moment, when it had built up all the energy possible, it came down smoothly and floated the ball to my brother. Underhand, and with no heat. Noel leaned in, twisted at the hip, and brought the bat swiftly over home plate. The aluminum tube made a quick swooshing sound followed by an explosion of laughter as Noel swung so hard that he almost fell over. Strike one. Everyone laughed but me.

"*Huele a ponche*, Noel," Mr. Villarreal yelled.

"What happened, *m'ijo*?" The eldest of the ladies called out from her chair. "*¿Quieres que le pegue yo?*"

My brother smiled and waved her off. "No, stay there. It won't happen again."

He stood with more conviction this time. Bat high in the air, legs apart and slightly bent. Fierce looking. *No way he's going to strike again, no way.* My father, with the full attention of our viewers, stood in his traditional pitcher's stance. The louder the fans shouted the longer it took for my dad to pitch the ball. "Sometime today!" I wanted to yell, but he threw it before I could. I could see its trajectory perfectly. *There is no way he'll miss this time.* Noel pulled back, lifted his left leg a little, then in one motion dropped it down and brought the bat forward. Swoosh. Strike two. More laughter.

I knew Noel's form. I studied it at his games while pressing my face against the fence. I even imitated it when I'd go up to bat. As I looked at him I realized that, if only slightly, his form was off. "What are you doing?" I shouted at him, but the screams from the church people, the opposing team, and even our team muffled my words. They continued laughing while I walked to first base where Leo stood coaching the runners.

"We have two runners on base."

"What's that, little guy?"

"I said there are two runners on base. What is he doing? How could he miss twice?"

Leo looked at me for a moment then lifted his sunglasses. He smiled with his eye, and placed his hand on my shoulder. "Check out your old man, Pete. He knows how to pitch."

My old man? The grey hair that stuck out from underneath my father's hat danced in the wind, and the creases on the side of his face came out more as he smiled. Miles of wrinkles covered the hand that held the softball against his thigh. In the distance I saw Villarreal holding up a spatula. He laughed, jumped, and yelled like a young man again. Full of fire. I thought about him, and my father working ten hour days. Then I remembered what my father had told me about playing hardball all his life. The ladies from the church yelled in the background about The Heat having to come out of retirement to finally strike out Noel. Their shouting didn't seem to get to my father, though. He stood on the mound, and stared at the strike zone.

The two runners we had on base didn't lead off, and my father didn't check if they had. Noel hit the bat against the plate, pulled up his shorts a little past his knees, and waited for the pitch. His eyes narrowed, and his bottom lip pressed against his teeth. When my father let go of the ball he didn't move back like I had seen so many other pitchers do. Everyone followed the ball on its way to home plate except for Noel and me. He kept his eyes on my father. I kept mine on him. Right before the ball reached the strike zone my brother smiled. Not a full teeth and eyes smile, but a small, almost unnoticeable one.

Swoosh. The dirt on home plate flew off, the yelling paused, and Noel's left arm almost came out of its socket as it tried to hold on to the bat. Strike three. It was only the end of the first inning yet both teams celebrated together. Hats flew in the air, and Noel had to fight off constant smacks to the head. *What happened, champ? He struck you out like a chump. You twisted like a ballerina on that last swing. Missed it by a mile.* Qué agüite. *You gonna cry? Hey,* pero *for reals. Your dad, man...your dad.*

Noel held his palms against his forehead and shook his head slowly, but beneath his hands I saw him smiling. "He got me," was all he said. We played a glorious game after that. I did my best at shortstop, and when someone teased me about missing a grounder I simply reminded them of Noel's strike out. Then we'd all laugh and imitate him twirling like a ballerina. We lost that day by two runs, but I didn't care. I was happy to see The Heat, even if he only struck out one person. As we walked off the field I came up next to Noel, and I asked him why he had done it.

"Do what?" he answered with the same smile he had flashed at home plate.

"...Nothing" I said, and left it at that.

Good Father

by Christine Granados

**PENING DAY IN ALAMO CITY'S FRESHLY RAKED** baseball field started with all the fanfare and cattiness of New York's fashion week. The tall, muscular teenage Bobcat infield worked the crowd with their opening-day razzle-dazzle. Dalton Reyes pitched the first ball of the season and everyone cheered as Junior Hernandez caught it and made a sharp throw to second that echoed. Second shot it to first, who threw the ball to third. The third baseman pitched it to shortstop and the entire infield ran it into Dalton and Junior. Behind the backstop, Ernesto Hernandez watched with the pride of a father and former player, who was used to being admired, as the team gathered around his oldest son, Junior. His younger son, Sergio stood at attention in the outfield with his teammates with his cap already over his heart. Ernesto thought, even though his youngest wasn't going to have the height of his older brother, he would have the speed that the eluded the eldest. Both kids surpassed even his skills when he was their age.

Baseball!

Bobcat head coach Steven Springer met the high school team on the mound where he took a microphone that was run out to him by the mayor's son. The young boy was given this privilege for his faithful attendance to Pony League practice, but Ernesto shook his head with the knowledge that Adam was on the field because of Sam Butler's position in town. Coach Springer read the Little League Pledge and called the Reverend Amit Gupta up to the mound to give the benediction. All the pomp and circumstance culminated with Sheila Jenkins singing "The Star Spangled Banner." Ernesto watched her father, Chad tear up. He knew Chad was thinking of the friends he had lost in Desert Storm. Sheila sounded just like she did on television when she sang at Kyle Stadium at the Aggie/Longhorn Thanksgiving day matchup. Although Sheila was quoted in *The Radio Dispatch* as saying she preferred larger crowds and the cold football weather to warm spring days, the high school senior said she was happy to practice the national anthem one more time before singing the song in her triple A debut in Round Rock the following week. Reading the article earlier that morning took Ernesto back to his Mexican League days. After the crowd cheered, the president of the little league, Lee Greene, walked to mound and said, "Play ball!" The crowd cheered some more and then dispersed.

Ernesto followed the Mudcats to the furthest of four identical fields to watch them warm up. He stood a few feet away from the first base dugout and rested his forearms over the chain link fence as the players stretched. He wondered why Coach Morgan wasn't walking them through these exercises. When Ernesto coached, he walked them through warm-up and made sure the team was thorough. These players were sloppy and slow about the whole affair. Ernesto rolled his eyes after seeing the coach in the dugout on his cell phone, and he worried that he had made a mistake allowing Sergio to decide which team he would play for this spring. The Mudcats took the field when the umpire shouted that they should play ball. This jarred Coach Morgan away from his phone conversation. He snapped his cell shut and put it in his pocket. Joe Leopold ran past Ernesto wearing khaki pants with dress shoes and slipping a black Mudcats' jersey over his Oxford shirt. The team skipped their infield warm-up, because these men thought more of work than the game. Ernesto decided he would talk to them after the game—teach a thing or two. By the second inning, Ernesto was gripping the chain link fence in anger because of the poor coaching.

He watched his son catch a line drive then pitch it underhanded to the second baseman for what could have been a double play. Sergio moved the ball from his black glove to his hand in one continuous motion. He was as practiced and studied as his father was at work when he lined up his mower to a distant marker at the start of a run. But Sergio's feet were an inch off the dirt as he threw, and this made the toss high. Ernesto hooked his callused fingers into the chain link fence and shook it.

He yelled in Spanish, "What's wrong with you, Sergio? Think!"

Sergio kept his eyes on the sand in front of him but nodded his head.

Coach Morgan yelled, "Shake it off, Serge, and be ready next time. It's coming to you."

Ernesto crossed his arms, rested them on his large hard belly, and watched the next batter. *I would have never put Chance Reyes on second base*, he thought. *The kid is too short. Chance should be playing third. He's quick and has a good arm.* Between Sergio and Chance nothing could get through to left field. If coached right, this team could go places.

Julie Reyes walked up to Ernesto and gave him an awkward sideways hug so their bellies wouldn't collide. She dropped the metal folding chair she carried and it shook the fence.

"Ernie, how are our boys doing?" she wheezed.

"They're ahead four to three with two outs in the second." Ernesto kept his eyes on the field as he spoke. "Sergio messed up a double play, but *Shance* brought a runner in with a pop fly to right field in the first inning."

"That's our boy!" Julie pumped her fist. "In the first game, too."

"Where's Octavio?" Ernesto touched his ear, and Sergio backpedaled from the dirt onto the grass.

"Tavie is working," Julie said, watching her son then Ernesto.

"*Muévete*," Ernesto sidestepped away from the coach in front of him to keep his line of sight clear. He grunted then said, "Working a double-shift?" He touched his ear again.

"You bet. With this one on the way, he's been pulling more and more of those." She pointed to her belly and watched Chance backup toward the grass, too.

"One more and you'll have an entire infield." Ernesto glanced at Julie. He smiled when he read on her black jersey "Baby Mudcat on Deck" that had a picture of a baseball bat underneath pointing to her belly.

"Yeah, yeah that's what Tavie says." She rubbed her belly. "And you could coach them all."

"I would. But..." He bent down and unfolded the metal chair for Julie.

"I don't understand. Why aren't you coaching this year?" She stepped in front of the chair so that the coach standing outside the dugout couldn't overhear.

"They won't let me." He pointed behind him toward a green concession stand.

"What? You mean Chad and Lee don't want you coaching?" She eyed the green hut behind her as if they could hear her from that distance.

"I don't understand either," Ernesto clapped when Sergio caught a deep pop fly and the team ran into the dugout. "My team went to the playoffs last year. And still they don't let me coach."

"Nice job, Mudcats! Way to go Serge!" Julie yelled and clapped. "You know about Chad and Lee, right?" she whispered.

"I know they run the league—" He clapped. "Come on Sergio, you've got this McGarrety. All his pitches are high and outside just the way you like them."

The coach stepped in Ernesto's line of sight and walked Sergio to the on deck circle as he took his place near third base.

"Perfect timing for me. It's the top of the lineup," Julie said.

"Good, he's telling him to take the first two pitches because McGarrety starts out wild."

"How do you know?" Julie waved her hand in her face like a fan.

"Everybody knows." Ernesto nodded his head and turned to Julie, whose freckled face was pink. "He held up two fingers. What else could he be saying?"

Julie giggled.

"What about Chad and Lee?" He leaned a forearm on the fence in front of him to watch the game.

"I went to high school with them." Julie placed both hands on the fence to steady herself.

"Yes and so did Octavio." He watched Sergio take the first pitch, which was high.

"Tavie was never at the parties like I was. Way to watch!" Julie yelled, as the second pitch sailed over the catcher's mitt and hit the backstop.

"Too bad there was nobody on base," Ernesto said.

"Chad and Lee are not very nice and…"

Sergio hit the third pitch shallow to center field.

Ernesto cupped his hands like megaphones and yelled. "Run, *m'ijo*, run fast, you can get a double. *Córrele, córrele*." He rubbed his hands across his chest. "Why did he hold him at first base? He could have made it to second. Carter throws high when he's in a hurry."

"Coach Morgan played ball in high school. I think he knows what he's doing," Julie said.

"He's never coached a championship team. I have." Ernesto shook his head. "I don't care if Chad and Lee are not nice. Some people say I'm not nice. Who needs nice?"

"They especially aren't nice to Mexicans, if you know what I mean." She patted her belly.

"Oh, you mean they're prejudiced?" He peered at the on deck circle. "Come on, Randy: pop it to left field."

"Yeah, if you want to call it that. How many Mexicans do you see coaching Pony League teams?" With cap in hand, Julie pointed to the field. "I've always thought that, and I've told Tavie."

"What does Octavio say?" Ernesto crossed his arms.

"He says I'm a chee... chee... chee something, but he doesn't know them like I do."

Ernesto laughed then leaned on the fence. "*Chinolera.* He should know; he works with them at the plant."

"Yeah, but I went to school with them. And they have always been and always will be," Julie said. "They were brutal to Sarah Contreras in high school."

"Sergio, you should have taken off the minute the pitcher winded up." Ernesto punched the fence before turning to Julie. "What do you mean?"

"They picked on her mercilessly." She clenched the fence. "They called her Sarah Colossal-ass."

"You talking about Miss Contreras, who lives on Travis Street?" He saw the ball hit the dirt in front of the catcher.

"The very one." Julie shook the fence. "Don't swing."

"I do her yard." He scratched his head. "You two are the same age?"

"No, she's two years younger than me."

"Ah, you're kidding." He turned and looked at Julie. "Colossal-ass? What does that mean?"

"Colossal, you know—massive, huge." She stretched her arms wide. "Oh, look: he got a piece of it."

Ernesto turned to watch Randy running toward first. "Tag up! Tag up, *m'ijo*!"

Julie cupped her mouth, "Go, go, go!"

"Why did he hit it to center? Sergio could have been tagged out." Ernesto shook his head.

"He swung late, is all," Julie said. "Way to advance the runner, Randy!"

"They're right, you know." Ernesto kicked at the fence as the next batter, Gustavo, planted his feet inside the batter's box. "It is pretty big."

She frowned then waved her hands in the air, as if trying to clear away a fly, "They're racist. Why else won't they let you coach? You're practically coaching from the sidelines." She took a deep breath and yelled, "Go, Gus!"

"Gustavo. It's Gustavo."

"That's what I said. Gus. Gus. Isn't that what I said?" She put her hands on her hips.

"It's Gustavo, Julia." Ernesto smiled.

She shook her head. "Oh, you and Tavie."

"What about me and Octavio?"

"Oh, Ernie, what's the big deal?"

Ernesto cleared his throat. "It's the name our—"

"Come on, Ernie, Ernie…" Julie cooed.

Ernesto laughed and pointed toward the field. "Gustavo is going to bunt. The coach should just let him hit. He knows what he's doing."

"Chance is up next. He wants more runners on the bases," Julie said.

"Yeah, you're probably right." He wiped sweat from his forehead with a finger. "I think it's because of last year. I had Adam Butler on my team, and he didn't start."

"Oh, really," Julie said. "Chad, Lee, and Sam go hunting in Colorado together every winter break."

"Yeah, I know. I like the kid, but everybody knows he's not a starter. Sam wanted me to start him. There was no way I was going to put Adam in. We were on a winning streak. Sam tried to tell me that his kid was as good as the Rodríguez and Placencio kids and I told him, 'Adam needs to practice more, to start.'"

Julie put her hand over her mouth to hide her laughter.

"I say to him, 'If you would get your glove on and go outside, spend some time teaching him how to field and catch pop flies, it would help him.'" Ernesto pointed above Julie's head.

"You didn't tell him that?" Julie blinked rapidly. "No wonder you're not coaching. Chad, Lee, and Sam are in Rotary, on the chamber board, and they go to church together."

"Yes, I did. And he tells me his son does come to practice." Ernesto kicked the fence and surveyed the field— he saw Sergio on third base and Gustavo on first. "You know that's not enough, right?"

Julie nodded her head in disbelief.

"So I said again, 'Adam needs to practice more.'" He stood erect and pointed four fingers at Julie. "'If want your son to be a good player, you need to be a good father and spend some time practicing with him.'"

Julie stared at the field. "Chance's up? What did I miss? Did Gus bunt?"

"Gustavo laid the ball down the third base line and beat the throw easy." Ernesto crossed his arms.

"Let's go, Chance. Hit it out of the park!" Julie clapped.

"You can't expect a kid to practice once or twice a week and then start." Ernesto hit the fence. "I think of the Rodríguez and Placencio kids and how often Gregorio and Estefan practice with them, and there was no way I was gonna start Adam."

"I can't believe you." Julie laughed and tried to watch her son.

"Take two, *Shance*. He's wild," Ernesto yelled. He turned to face Julie and blocked her view of home plate. "So Sam's face is red and he's standing so close to me that I can smell the pickle on his breath. I have my hands across my chest like this with my catcher's mitt on."

Julie stared at Ernesto's bare hands.

He stepped so close to Julie that their round bellies touched. "He's real close so I tap him on the face with it."

"You hit him?" Her eyes widened.

"No." He shook his head. "I tapped him on the face, like this."

"Ouch!" Julie took an unbalanced step back and sat down in her lawn chair.

"You're all right." Ernesto crouched on one knee. "He was standing too close and I just gave him a little tap to back him up like you just did. You know how tall he is, and he was standing over me. I'm not gonna let anybody get up in my face, ever. I told him, 'I'll do it again if you don't back up.'"

Julie was silent as she touched her face.

The crowd in the stands yelled. "Go, Chance! Home run! Home run! Run, Chance!"

Julie peered at Ernesto out of the corner of her eye. She whispered, "I think it's a home run."

"No, it's a triple." Ernesto leaned a hand on the chain link. "If Chance were a little bit faster he'd make it. Rubén's arm can snag even Gustavo from center field."

"Oh, what do you know?" She rubbed her cheek and watched the left fielder make a perfect throw to the catcher as Chance rounded third.

You'll Hit It over Anzaldúas Bridge

by Robert Paul Moreira

The Anzaldúas International Bridge opened for traffic at 6 a.m. on Tuesday, Dec. 15, 2009. It serves as the most direct and efficient route between the Rio Grande Valley and Mexican cities such as Monterrey and Mexico City. The bridge spans 3.2 miles.

—City of McAllen, Texas, website

I am not afraid.

—Gloria Anzaldúa, *Borderlands*

OU'LL SLAP IT. SHOCK IT. POP IT. ROCK IT. Smooth. Yeah, smooth. And then *CRACK!* And you'll make it go *arriba* a little and into the sky, up and over the parking lot, and watch it land close to where the *pochos* and Mexes and Winter Texans all slouch in line and the BPs stare like Oakleyed hawks and carry black, shiny guns. You'll duck down when all those heads turn to see where the failed meteor came from, and so will Chuy and the rest of the gang behind you. Next to Julia, rubbing a shoulder against hers, pretending not to look into her cotton-white, teenie face, you'll giggle too, act suave beside the daughter of Teresa, your next door neighbor, and Clifford, the ex-cop from Boston who RVed down one winter and slummed in your barrio with Julia's mom and liked it so much he decided to stay. Caught up connecting her cute freckles you'll think about the next time you'll burn *hacia adentro* when you go over to her house to see Julia and how Clifford'll be there.

And it's not so much his eyes you'll hate when you walk in again, his eyes that you know have always fixed on your tits that you once tried to wrap tight like Gwyneth Paltrow did in *Shakespeare in Love* in front of your mirror a few times, that *pinche* mirror that shows you to you with fury, but then it all turned out as useless as pushing Mayan pyramids into sacred ground, so since then you conceded defeat and let them hang loose, no bra, freer than freer than free, just to make a statement, until Julia told you that other fine day that she did the same thing too, and sealed it with a kiss.

Nah. Not that. You'll think of that other power Clifford's got over you. His *poder* when he speaks. You'll think of asking *Is Julie home?* clear and proper, followed by Clifford's owning of your body with his eyes again, and his answer back in Spanish that you won't understand in its entirety: *Julia está en su cuarto, machorra.* And then his laugh. His long laugh that seems to go on forever like the Palm Sunday Mass you always hate attending with your mother, the Palmview saint, who never fails to tell God and then you *cambia...please change.* But even Clifford's laugh never bites as hard as knowing his words have eyes that look down on you, talk down to you, and that even if you were to respond with a *Kiss my ass!* or *Screw you, you white piece of shit!* it wouldn't matter. It wouldn't matter. It wouldn't matter. You'll wish you knew Spanish good enough to tell him something fierce like that, and you'll blame your mother for failing to give you her native tongue because it was her fault for not showing you, the curse words at the very least, but then all those thoughts will disappear. *Julie's in her room,*

Clifford'll say, as nice as he's always been bad from the beginning, and you'll watch the skin around his eyes sag so that if he laughed at that instant you'd know, you'd know deep down that he'd crumble like a dried up castle made up of South Padre sand. He'll move to the side, forget you're even there, and finally you'll walk in.

In her bedroom, you'll thank *los santos* and *santas* that Julia always makes up for everything you go through before getting there. You'll think of how she's mostly English too, speaks but a speck of Spanish, and is much lighter in skin tone than you, like you're the burned part of the tortilla while she's the inside; and how getting close to her is also a language, your language with her, a language of love, where the both of you can communicate without any interference from the outside world. You'll smile when you see yourself in her mirror because it's always much more polite than yours, and the crazy thought of undressing in front of it and taking in the sights of all that God gave you, really taking them in and being proud of the whorls of flesh that make up your body, all of that will cross your mind. Unbuttoning your shirt you'll look over at Julia, feet crossed with her cute pink toenails and staring up at you from the comfort of her bed, and you'll reconsider. *Not yet*, you'll say to yourself. *Not yet*. You'll cuddle up next to her and watch TV instead. You'll hold her hand and let the sweat build in between. She will too. The world will turn slowly with both of you on it, but you won't even know it's there.

In the present, you'll look up to make sure the coast is clear, and the others will follow your example. Chuy'll play the role of your biggest fan at the moment, and he'll praise you with a flurry of words packed into a sentence and followed by the word *"buey,"* and you'll use the word too, not worried about what it means because you've never heard Clifford use it, but you'll remember your *Tío* Armando who said that word all the time too, your *tío* with the cleft lip and missing his uvula from birth so that when he spoke it seemed as if God had assigned him a personal demon to eternally pinch his nose. You could talk to him about demons, you'll think, then smile. *What's boo-ey?* Julia will ask, and everyone will laugh until you wave your bat at them, and then Chuy will tell her it's the same as "dude" or "bro" when speaking in Mexicano. *Booey!* Julia will say again, cute, and this time no one will laugh. After a wink she'll stand there tall, like a wall you'll want to climb over, but you'll hold yourself back, feeling like a million bucks and twice that in *pesos*. You'll tell Chuy it's time for the next one, and he'll nod, and the rest of the guys will back away. A kiss for Julia, and then you'll pat her on the ass, MLB-style, for everyone to see, and see they will, and you'll watch her join the guys a few feet away. You'll feel a strength in your soul, *hacia adentro*, inside your body and in your arms like never before, and the expanse of silky blue sky above you will seem conquerable all of a sudden, and the moment made just for you. You'll yell out in confidence *You see the sky?* and the guys and Julia will say *Yeah! Yeah!* You'll go on: *See the clouds? See the space between them? Those holes in the firmament of* el cielo? They'll nod and agree, saying *¡Sí! Yes! ¡Sí!* and at that moment you'll know. You'll finally know. You'll know it as deep as the blood inside you. Chuy'll swing his arm back and toss that hard piece of *caliche* your way and you'll time it, bring around your *bate* and smack it and get this one good, as good as ever, all sweet spot, *cabrona*, and you'll hit this one far, farther than ever, and it'll fly up and *arriba* like an ancestral spirit on fire and set free, over everyone, over everything, over men and women and *pocho*, Mex, and border-patrolled flesh and occupied earth and pissed-in water. On a heavenly arc. High. Up and over that brilliant bridge. And you'll imagine the rock finally falling on the other side and rolling, tumbling on its belly across the unpaved Reynosa streets to the feet of hungry children selling gum for five *pesos* or *¡Alarma!* magazines with full-color photos of their fathers' severed heads stuffed tight in Igloo coolers bought in the EE. UU. You'll feel like a crumpled dollar smoothed out as best as possible for the Coke machine, but still rejected.

Still rejected.

Then everyone around you will cheer. Then a silence. Julia will come close. You'll stand there with her, with everyone else around you, like in a ceremony, watching, praying, hoping. Waiting. Waiting for that special someone on the other side who'll take the chance and hit it back.

Contributor Biographies

PETER C. BJARKMAN is widely acknowledged as the leading authority on pre-and post-revolution Cuban baseball history and has travelled extensively in Cuba, as well as watching the Cuban national team in most international tournaments since 1996. He is the author of *A History of Cuban Baseball, 1864-2006* (McFarland, 2007) and has been senior writer for the website www.BaseballdeCuba.com for the past seven years. Born in Hartford, Connecticut, and residing in Lafayette, Indiana, Bjarkman holds a PhD in Spanish Linguistics (University of Florida) but retired from academia in 1987 to pursue a full-time writing career. He was recently featured with celebrity chef Anthony Bourdain on the Travel Channel episode of "No Reservations Cuba."

NORMA ELIA CANTÚ serves as professor of US Latin@ Studies at the University of Missouri, Kansas City; she has published widely in the areas of folklore, literary, women's, and border studies. She edits two book series (*Literatures of the Americas* for Palgrave, *Rio Grande/Rio Bravo* for Texas A&M Press) and thus fosters the publication of critical scholarship on Latinas and Latinos. Her numerous publications include the award-winning novel *Canícula: Snapshots of a Girlhood en la Frontera* that chronicles her coming of age in Laredo, Texas. She is cofounder of *CantoMundo*, a space for Latin@ poets, and a member of the Macondo Writers Workshop; her creative work has appeared in *Vandal*, *Prairie Schooner*, and *Feminist Studies Journal* among many other venues.

PETE CAVA is a native Staten Islander and a Fordham University graduate who lives in Indianapolis. He worked as media information officer for the Amateur Athletic Union from 1974-1979 and for USA Track & Field from 1980-1998. Currently the CEO of International Sports Associates, Cava worked with Team Italy at the 2006 World Baseball Classic and with Team Venezuela in 2009. He served as a deputy venue press chief for the 2013 WBC in Fukuoka and Tokyo, Japan. Cava is the author of *Mom's Handy Book of Backyard Games* and *Tales from the Cubs Dugout*. He is currently working on *The Encyclopedia of Indiana-Born Major League Baseball Players*.

THOMAS DE LA CRUZ is an author from Elsa, Texas, who writes about the small town that has inspired even smaller stories. He is currently working on his MFA at the University of Texas-Pan American.

NELSON DENIS was a New York State Assemblyman. A graduate of Harvard College and Yale Law School, he wrote over 300 editorials as the editorial director of *El Diario/La Prensa*, and won the "Best Editorial Writing Award" from the *National Association of Hispanic Journalists*. Nelson published poetry in the *Harvard Advocate*; features in the *Harvard Political Review*; and editorials in the *New York Daily News, New York Sun,* and *New York Newsday*. His screenplays won awards from the *New York Foundation for the Arts* and the *New York State Council on the Arts*. Nelson wrote/directed the feature film comedy *Vote For Me!* which premiered at the

Tribeca Film Festival, won numerous film festival awards, and received nationwide media coverage.

DAGOBERTO GILB is the award-winning author of *Before the End, after the Beginning*. His previous books are *The Flowers, Gritos, Woodcuts of Women, The Last Known Residence of Mickey Acuña*, and *The Magic of Blood*.

CHRISTINE GRANADOS was born and grew up in El Paso, Texas. She has been a Spur Award finalist and winner of the 2006 Alfredo Cisneros del Moral Foundation Award from the Macondo Foundation. Christine's fiction and nonfiction has appeared in *Evergreen Review, Callaloo*, NPR's *Latino USA, Texas Monthly, Texas Observer, El Andar*, and others. It has been anthologized in several college textbooks and anthologies, including *NewBorder: Contemporary Voices from the Texas/Mexico Border, The Story and Its Writer: An Introduction to Short Fiction, Texas: A Case Study, Literary El Paso*, and *Camino del Sol: Fifteen Years of Latina and Latino Writing*. Granados received a BA in journalism from UT El Paso and an MFA in creative writing from Texas State University. Before joining the faculty at Texas Tech University she taught at the University of Houston-Victoria and Texas A&M University. Editor at *Moderna* and *Hispanic* magazines for several years, she worked as journalist for the *El Paso Times, Austin American-Statesman, Rockdale Reporter*, and *People Magazine*.

JUAN ANTONIO GONZÁLEZ is a narrator, a poet and a literary critic. His academic works have been published in a diversity of learned journals from the U.S., Latin America, and Spain. He has published poetry and prose in the following volumes: *Itineransias*, *Letras en el Estuario*, *Antología Canicular*, *Voces desde el Casamata*, *Encuentro de poesía Río Grande/ Río Bravo*, *Antología Invernal*, and *Antología de poesía sobre poesía*. He is a professor of Hispanic Letters, Creative Writing and Translation at the University of Texas at Brownsville. Since 1996 he has served as editor-in-chief of the literary journals *Novosantanderino* and *De Puño y Letra,* while holding editorial appointments in the journals *Puentes* (Arizona State University) and *Pegaso* (University of Oklahoma at Norman).

MELISSA HIDALGO is an Assistant Professor in English and World Literature at Pitzer College in Claremont, CA. Her research and teaching areas include Chicana/o literature and cultural production, queer Chicana/o literature and performance, cultural studies, and popular music fandom. She also teaches classes about sports and literature. A true-blue Los Angeles Dodgers fan, Hidalgo also has a soft spot for the Chicago Cubs. And she believes in the practice of writing for the soul. She considers it a privilege to count Cherríe Moraga, Adelina Anthony, and Sharon Bridgforth among her teachers and artistic inspirations.

KATHRYN LANE writes both fiction and poetry. Her short stories have been published in *The Texas A&M Border Fiction Anthology* and *Swirl Literary*. Originally from Mexico, her writing is inspired by Latin American cultures. She performs poetry in both English and Spanish. Kathryn's poems have appeared in the *Austin International Poetry Festival Anthology (2012 and 2013 editions); Homeless Diamonds*, a London-based journal; *Primitive Archer*; and *Swirl*. Two books with her poetry, *A Conversation on India* and *Spirit Rocks*, were published in 2012. The Friendswood Public Library featured her poems when their Blog showcased the Rothko Chapel and Mark Rothko's art. Kathryn is a board member of Montgomery Literary Arts Council.

ROBERT PAUL MOREIRA received his MFA from the University of Texas-Pan American in 2010. Currently, he is an English PhD candidate at the University of Texas-San Antonio researching alterity and constructed identities in sports fiction, films, and performance. His fiction, interviews, criticism, and scholarship have been published or are forthcoming in a variety of venues, including *Southwest American Literature*, *Soccer and Society*, *Bluestem*, *Aethlon: Journal of Sports Literature*, *Storyglossia*, and the anthologies *SOL: Vol. I* (SOL, 2012) and *New Border Writing* (Texas A&M Press, 2013). He is the recipient of a Pushcart Prize nomination (2012), two graduate fiction awards from the Texas Association of Creative Writing Teachers (2009, 2010), and the Wendy Barker Creative Writing Award (2011). He teaches writing and literature at the University of Texas-Pan American.

WAYNE RAPP was born and raised in the border town of Bisbee, Arizona, and traces his Mexican roots to the Figueroa and Valenzuela families of Sonora. He is a graduate of the University of Arizona with a major in English. His fiction has appeared in various publications including *Americas Review, Grit, THEMA, Vincent Brothers Review,* and *High Plains Literary Review*. His story, "In the Time of Marvel and Confusion," was nominated for a Pushcart Prize, and he has twice been honored with fellowships from the Ohio Arts Council. His collection of border stories, *Burnt Sienna*, was a finalist for the 2005 Miguel Mármol Prize for Fiction. In "Chasing Chato," he mixes his fictional protagonist with real baseball players of the era.

DAVID RICE was born in Weslaco, Texas, in 1964 and raised in Edcouch, Texas. He is the author of *Give the Pig a Chance, Crazy Loco,* and *Heart Shaped Cookies*. His stories have appeared in several anthologies and are taught in schools and universities across Texas.

DANIEL ROMO is the author of the book of prose poems, *When Kerosene's Involved* (Black Coffee Press). His poetry and photography can be found in the *Los Angeles Review, Gargoyle, MiPOesias, Yemessee*, and elsewhere. He earned an MFA in Creative Writing from Queens University of Charlotte, and he leads off and plays a stellar outfield for the

Long Beach Barons. He lives in Long Beach, CA, and at danielromo.net.

RENÉ SALDAÑA, JR. is the author of several YA books, including *The Jumping Tree*, *Finding Our Way: Stories*, *The Whole Sky Full of Stars*, and *The Good Long Way*. He also writes the Mickey Rangel, Private Detective series, a bilingual flip book for the young reader. Saldaña recently co-edited *¡Juventud!*, an anthology of fiction and poetry about growing up on borders. He lives in Lubbock, TX, with his wife and children, where he teaches in the College of Education at Texas Tech University.

Born in East L.A., California, in 1973, **EDWARD VIDAURRE** writes poetry about his upbringing and experiences of living in the barrio. Raised in Boyle Heights in the projects of Aliso Village, his poetry takes you through his memory of La Lucha. Known to his friends as Barrio Poet, Vidaurre says:" Sometimes the barrio claims us, holds us by our feet like roots in its field of chalk outlines closed off by the screaming yellow tape being pulled from its soul." Vidaurre is the founder of Pasta, Poetry & Vino and Barrio Poet Productions. He has been nominated for a Pushcart Prize for his poem "Lorca in the Barrio" and also is co-editing an anthology called *Twenty* in memory of Newtown, Connecticut, through El Zarape Press with Daniel Garcia Ordaz, Katie Hoerth, and José Chapa V. His first collection of poetry, *I Took My Barrio on a Road-trip*, was published by Slough Press.

Other Titles from

VAO Publishing

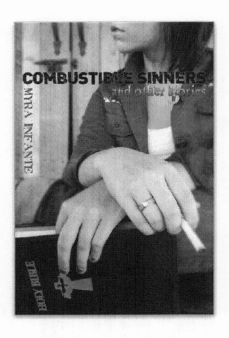

Combustible Sinners and Other Stories by Myra Infante
ISBN: 9780615556703

Lissi Linares is a pastor's daughter whose love for others contrasts with
her fear of eternal damnation. Little Jasmine "Jazzy Moon" Luna is
determined to save Jesus from being crucified. Naida Cervantes hides a
brutal secret behind shapeless, florid dresses. Hermana Gracie tries to set
her son up with a good Christian girlfriend, only to make a surprising
discovery. Zeke wants a new guitar and Ben wants a cool girlfriend, but
what they find as migrant workers in Arkansas changes their desires.
These individuals and others try to negotiate the often rocky intersection
of faith and culture in seven independent but intertwining tales that
explore life in an evangelical Christian, Mexican-American community.
Frank, funny and heart-breakingly real, this volume explores themes of
identity, culture, religion and sexuality in the context of a little-known
subset of Hispanic culture.

¡Juventud! *Growing up on the Border*
Edited by René Saldaña, Jr., and Erika Garza-Johnson

ISBN: 9780615778259

Borders are magical places, and growing up on a border, crossing and recrossing that space where this becomes that, creates a very special sort of person, one in whom multiple cultures, languages, identities and truths mingle in powerful ways. In these eight stories and sixteen poems, a wide range of authors explore issues that confront young people along the US-Mexico border, helping their unique voices to be heard and never ignored.

Featuring the work of David Rice, Xavier Garza, Jan Seale, Guadalupe García McCall, Diane Gonzales Bertrand, and many others.

Mexican Bestiary | *Bestiario Mexicano*
by Noé Vela and David Bowles
ISBN: 9780615571195

Who protects our precious fields of corn? What leaps from the darkness when you least suspect it? Which spirit waits for little kids by rivers and lakes? From the ahuizotl to the xocoyoles—and all the imps, ghosts and witches in between—this illustrated bilingual encyclopedia tells you just what you need to know about the things that go bump in the night in Mexico and the US Southwest.

¿Quién protege nuestras milpas preciosas? ¿Qué cosa salta de la oscuridad cuando menos te lo esperes? ¿Cuál espíritu acecha a los pequeños cerca de los ríos y los lagos? Desde el ahuizotl a los xocoyoles—y demás diablillos, fantasmas y brujas—esta enciclopedia ilustrada bilingüe te dice justo lo que debes saber sobre las cosas que dan miedo en México y en el suroeste de los Estados Unidos.

Made in the USA
Lexington, KY
07 May 2014